''Slocum, come out of there with your damn hands in the air!'' the voice shouted, and the words echoed back four times.

''You're weighing down our patience. Come on out!'' The other man's sentence was punctuated with a high-powered rifle report and the scream of a ricocheted bullet off a flat rock high up the slope.

Slocum smiled to himself as he mounted his dun horse. Lyle and Dirk Abbot would soon grow tired of their game and rush his hideout. They were sure in for a rude awakening—he wasn't up there.

Slocum paused and searched the mountainside. He could see the puffs of smoke rise from their rifles as they charged up the slope to take him.

''Sorry, boys, I'm heading for Utah . . .''

DON'T MISS THESE
ALL-ACTION WESTERN SERIES
FROM THE BERKLEY PUBLISHING GROUP

THE GUNSMITH by J. R. Roberts
Clint Adams was a legend among lawmen, outlaws, and ladies.
They called him . . . the Gunsmith.

LONGARM by Tabor Evans
The popular long-running series about U.S. Deputy Marshal
Long—his life, his loves, his fight for justice.

SLOCUM by Jake Logan
Today's longest-running action Western. John Slocum rides a
deadly trail of hot blood and cold steel.

JAKE LOGAN

THE ARIZONA STRIP WAR

JOVE BOOKS, NEW YORK

THE ARIZONA STRIP WAR

A Jove Book / published by arrangement with
the author

PRINTING HISTORY
Jove edition / January 1997

The Putnam Berkley World Wide Web site address is
http://www.berkley.com/berkley

ISBN: 0-515-11997-0

A JOVE BOOK®
Jove Books are published by The Berkley Publishing Group,
200 Madison Avenue, New York, New York 10016.
JOVE and the "J" design are trademarks
belonging to Jove Publications, Inc.

PRINTED IN THE UNITED STATES OF AMERICA

10 9 8 7 6 5 4 3 2 1

1

1873—Western Colorado.

Bent over with the horse's hoof in his lap, Slocum wedged the point of his large skinning knife under the horse's shoe. At first the plate held fast, so he pried it back and forth to loosen it. He turned to listen to the pair talking on the mountain above him. Then, satisfied they were still occupied, he returned to the task at hand. He worked feverishly until the nails began to pull loose from the rim of the hoof. Soon the space between the iron and the bottom of the animal's foot became an ever-widening gap, until at last he wrenched the shoe free.

Then with dedication he began to shave away the animal's hoof until the knife got dangerously close to the blood vessels. A telltale pile of white shavings was around the horse's hoof after he released it.

A rifle shot whined over the mountaintop above him. He drew his neck inside the collar of his shirt at the report.

"Slocum, come out of there with your damn hands in

the air!'' the voice shouted, and the words echoed back four times.

"You're weighing down our patience. Come on out!" The other man's sentence was punctuated with a high-powered rifle report and the scream of a ricocheted bullet off a flat rock high up the slope.

Slocum moved to the other horse standing hipshot under the saddle.

"Easy, big boy," he said as he ran his hand down the horse's rump and lifted the beast's rear leg. A grin crossed his face as he plunged the knife's tip easily under the shoe and pried the plate half free in his first attempt.

He listened to the pair talking about rushing the position above them on the mountain. They were out of his sight, about two hundred yards up the mountain from their horses and Slocum. He bent over again and began to shave the bottom of this horse's hoof down almost to the quick before he released it.

Then he used the razor-sharp edge of the knife to score the mohair girths under the stirrups so they would be less conspicuous. That task completed, he cut their pack mule's lead rope and with a slap on the hip sent the skittery animal down the narrow path through the house-high boulders that led to the stream below.

Both horseshoes in his hand, he turned his head and listened as more rifle shots struck the outcroppings on the mountain. The same formation that the Abbot brothers thought still housed Slocum. He smiled to himself as he mounted his dun horse. Lyle and Dirk Abbot would soon grow tired of their game and rush his hideout. They were sure in for a rude awakening—he wasn't up there.

Slocum hurried the dun downhill. He arrived in time to see the black mule dive into the stream in a great silver splash, pitch his way across the knee-deep water, and then, breaking wind like a bean bandit, the mule clamored up the far bank. He headed into the cedars, bucking like a house afire. Shouldn't take long—Slocum felt certain before the mule went a quarter mile he would have everything the Abbots owned scattered out to the four winds

Slocum paused and searched the mountainside. He could see the puffs of smoke rise from their rifles as they charged up the slope to take him.

"Sorry, boys, I'm heading for Utah," he said softly to himself, and sent the dun into the river. By the time Lyle and Dirk Abbot learned that he had slipped off the mountain, turned their pack mule loose, took a shoe off each of their horses, shaved down their hooves to the quick, and had ridden away, they would be fit to be tied. And this would be long before they mounted up and their girths gave way.

"I sure hate to treat bounty hunters that way," he said aloud as the dun scrambled up the far bank, shook the water like a dog, and then the abbots struck out to the west. "But some of them never learn when to quit."

The afternoon sun shone a bloody light on the snow-covered peaks of the Rockies behind them. It would require weeks before the greedy pair ever found a trace of his trail, and by then he planned to be far, far away. He rose in the stirrups and set the dun into a trot.

Riding on at sundown, he kept to the timber, skirting a store-and-ranch combination. From the trees he could see several horses hipshot at the rack; obvious this business served as a gathering place. It would be the first place the two brothers would head. Holding up their reward posters and posing as U.S. marshals, they would interrogate every man in the place. Except no one would have seen the man in the crude ink drawing who could be any one of a thousand people on the frontier.

He crossed into Utah two days later, using a series of dim animal trails through the sagebrush. He rode as due west as the terrain would allow. Without a marker he had little idea of the location of the actual boundary, but felt he had ridden far enough by then to be in the next state. Sometime around midday he struck a stream. The diamond glare from the clear water rushing away under the fluttering cotton woods encouraged him to dismount and consider a bath.

State lines, he knew, meant little to bounty men like the Abbots, but it put him farther from their greedy hands. So far he had avoided anyone seeing him, and he had not stopped anyplace for supplies or to ask for directions. There had been lots of windswept and rocky surfaces for miles to hide his horse's prints. He never directly crossed a stream, forcing any pursuers to ride up and down the banks to discover where he had left the water.

Satisfied he was alone, he hung his gun belt on the saddle horn as the dun busied himself grazing. He loosened the girth and patted the horse on the neck. He was a solid pony and he appreciated the animal's efforts.

"You get some good grass in your belly and I'll dip in the water awhile before we head on." He left the horse chomping on the fresh graze and went to the edge of the stream. The hole of water under the cut bank looked deep enough to come to his waist. He sat on the ground to remove his boots and considered the latest turn in fortune.

"You've got to ride out of here," Evangeline Jordan had said as she hung over the top bar of the high corral fence, her face flushed from the exertion of a wild buckboard ride from town. "Two men that call themselves the Abbot brothers, from Fort Scott, Kansas, are in town asking about you. They've got a reward poster. Slocum, will you go saddle a horse right now! Please, for me. I'll go fix something for you to eat on the trail."

He raised the whip and the three-year-old threw his ears forward and looked aside at him as he trotted around the pen in a circle. When he pointed the whip at him, on command the bloodred colt began to short-lope.

"Did you hear me?" she said in an out-of-breath screech.

"I hear good." He remained intent on the animal he was training. "Did these two look tough?"

"They looked like bears, beards and all. Do you know them?"

He nodded and whistled to the colt. He slid to a perfect stop, hind feet under him, and whirled to head for Slocum.

"What did you ever do in Kansas to get them after you?" she asked.

"There isn't any limitation on a murder warrant."

"How old is it?" She frowned from her perch on the corral fence.

"Maybe seven years ago." He reached out and touched the colt's muzzle. "Those two once came to Montana looking for me. Some of my drover friends sent them to an unfriendly Indian camp, even described the tepee to them as the one I would be in." He began to laugh aloud at the recollection.

"What's so funny?" she demanded at his laughter.

"It actually belonged to some chief who had just married a new bride. The Abbots came busting in, well, the old chief must have been right in the middle of his honeymoon and they were soon outside, and as I understand had several arrows in their backsides to be removed when they finally got back to Miles City."

"They looked tough enough in town."

"They are. I need to lead them off and permanently lose them," he said, stripping the halter off the colt and heading for the gate.

"You know I hate you leaving." She rushed over and hugged him. He held the widow Jordan tight, letting her full breasts press into his chest. He would miss her too.

"They give you any trouble—"

"They won't. I'll have a couple of the boys stay around close the next few weeks. And the colts. You were getting along so good with them."

"Another few weeks, you'd had some fine broke cow ponies for the remuda," he agreed with a disappointed shake of his head. The string of young horses had been his to gentle-break and they all were close to being ridable.

"Maybe Shorty can finish up on them?" she wondered aloud.

"You'll need someone with more patience," he warned her as he doubted the bowlegged cowboy might be the best choice.

"You pick him, then."

"It ain't my business—"

She reached up pulled his face down to hers and began to kiss him on the mouth. A wave of nausea spread though his guts at the thought of having to leave her lusty ways. The notion of parting with the widow curdled his stomach further when he tasted the alkali on her mouth and then sipped on the honey from her tongue. No time left to love her voluptuous body that fit so well under him each time they made love. Damn bounty hunters anyway . . .

Stripped of his clothing to take his bath in the stream, he checked to be certain the grazing horse was all right, and satisfied, he waded into the water. The shocking chill almost forced him to climb out, but instead he headed for his place to bathe in the swirling waist-deep water.

Soon he got accustomed to the cold and he briskly used handfuls of sand from the bottom to rub the dirt from his skin, then rinsed it away. Clean at last, he waded to the shore, the light wind drying him so fast, it caused goose bumps to rise on his back. A quick survey of the bank— nothing in sight—and he climbed out and gathered his clothes to wash them. The warm sun of the early fall day beat down on his bare skin as he scrubbed the grime from his pants, shirt, underwear, and socks in the stream's rushing water.

His clothing finally hung atop various bushes to dry, he sat on a large rock and absorbed the heat. He wasn't ready for the Indian that rode up from the west on a thin paint horse. The man appeared almost without warning, and Slocum was forced to snatch up his pants and dress in record time—though nudity never bothered an Indian, it did him. The wet britches were a struggle to pull on.

Barefoot, he went quickly for his gun belt and strapped it on in case of trouble as the old man crossed the stream. Two women appeared on the far bank, and they both carried babies on boards. Bare to the waist, they set down their papooses, removed their skirts, and began to wade the stream in the altogether, carrying their children in their arms.

"Ho," the man said. His face was sun-darkened and wrinkled, but his eyes were steady as an eagle's. He wore one long, greasy feather stuck in a bandanna that was wrapped around his head. His clothing was a mixture of threadbare white man's pants and shirt.

"Ho," Slocum said, raising his right arm in a sign of peace.

"Where you go, white man?"

"Salt Lake City on a mission," Slocum said to throw the man off and perhaps make him believe that he was a Mormon on a holy trip.

"You got food?"

"Jerky."

The man twisted in the saddle and said something sharp to the two women. They put down their papooses and hurried forward, still naked as Eve. The flat-nosed one was of broad build, her long breasts tight with milk. The thinner one had large nipples over small puddles of flesh.

"Which one you want?" he demanded.

Slocum shook his head. "I have some jerky. We all eat."

The man shook his head. "Got too many gawdamn wives, you take one. You no have one."

"Have wife many miles." Slocum pointed to the west.

"Many wives?" the buck asked, frowning.

"Many wives," Slocum said. This chief might as well believe he had a dozen. Neither of the squaws interested him; he dug out the jerky and handed him several pieces, then gave some to each of the women, who both grinned, showing several black spaces where their teeth were missing.

The Indian dismounted and gave the rein to the fat squaw. He hunkered down beside Slocum as if they were some sort of old friends and chewed lustily on the dry, sun-browned meat. They were obviously Paiutes, the kind that some folks called Digger Indians. These people had few possessions and lived on such things as grasshoppers in season.

Slocum also knew they were great thieves and it would be three against one after dark if he remained. He looked on as the Indian made a great effort to swirl the dry bites of jerky around inside his mouth to sop up any spittle as he chewed on it.

"You sleep with her." The chief pointed to the thin one.

Slocum shook his head and went on masticating his jerky. He had no intention of sleeping with either of the women. Having finished eating, Slocum put on his boots, shirt, and vest, and cinched up the saddle girth. When he jerked down the stirrup, the thinner woman was so close to him, he could smell her rank musk. She tried to take his hand and place it on her body; when he refused, she looked up with her pitiful eyes.

He ignored her and swung into the saddle.

"You no-good sum bitch!" she swore, and then she rushed in and tried to kick at his horse.

The dun reined around handily and avoided her attempted insulting footwork. Slocum sent him into the river and never looked back until he reached the far side. When he did turn in the saddle, both women were bent over and pointing their copper rumps at him as well as indicating toward that portion of their anatomy in an obscene way. Still squatted on the ground, the Indian chewed on his jerky. Slocum turned back, rose in the saddle, and trotted the dun toward the sunset.

A cooler north wind found him a few days later. He rode off into a small community and purchased a canvas jumper for warmth at a log store. Besides the stiff new coat, he bought some dry beans, a block of hard cheese, crackers, and a few oranges. The store was run by a small man with black hair parted in the middle, and wearing an unsoiled white apron. Like Slocum suspected, there was no coffee, tea, or tobacco for sale—all prohibited items on the Mormon church's list. He felt lucky that he had rationed his small cigars for occasional treats.

"What else, sir?" the man asked.

Slocum surveyed his purchases and shook his head. Nothing more. He turned as a tall woman in a blue dress entered the store.

"Oh, Sister Butler, I shall be right with you," he said.

"Thank you, Brother Morton," she said, and acted interested in a pile of ready-made brogans on a table near the front door.

Her beauty made Slocum search his past. Where did he know such a handsome woman from? He wanted to steal another look at Sister Butler. Something was familiar about her—he wished for another view. The store was dark and the frugal merchant was busy adding the purchases up on the butcher paper. Obviously, he was too thrifty to burn lamps during the day despite the lack of natural light.

"Comes to four dollars ten cents, sir."

Slocum paid and thanked him. With the new coat tucked under his arm and in the other hand a cotton poke that the man had placed his purchases in, he turned for another glimpse of the woman.

Faye Arnold was her maiden name, he felt certain. But her blue eyes never wavered as he turned sideways to allow her to pass.

"Good day, sir," she said so impersonally, for an instant he doubted his own memory.

"What for you today, Sister Butler?" the man asked.

Slocum gave her shapely derriere a last good look, then he went outside. The buckboard and ranch horse team hitched at the rail was obviously hers. She had come in from the west; he planned to ride west. Perhaps he could stop her somewhere out of sight of the town folks and they could talk about old times.

Since he rode in, he knew he had caught the eye of several gossiping women who were hanging clothes out to dry. A stranger in town, a drifter passing through, always drew hard looks as the natives speculated on his probable identity. Faye Arnold, he repeated to himself as he booted the dun horse into a long trot. No sign of the Abbot brothers in days, they were no doubt back to cold-trailing him—or had returned to Fort Scott, he hoped to stay.

The notion of Faye Arnold's long, honey-colored hair spilled all over him. Ogallala, Nebraska—that was where he caught the man who'd robbed her daddy of their cattle moneys. The Pike Hotel—that was where she slipped up-stairs after midnight and rapped softly on his door.

"Does your father know where you are?" he had asked in a whisper as he let her in the room, holding a blanket around his waist to cover himself. Damn, he hoped the man didn't ever learn his daughter's destiny as a chill of concern ran up his spine.

"Silly, no." She laughed out loud and took his face in her hands to kiss him as he jammed the door shut, still trying to hold the blanket up to shield his state of undress. "I come to show you how much I appreciate your helping my daddy get that money back."

"How old are you?" he asked.

"Eighteen," she said, and let her face shake away his concerns as she unpinned the long ribbons of her golden hair.

"Why, you ain't a day older than fifteen."

"Hush, these walls are thinner than paper," she said, and began to unbutton her bodice. "I was eighteen a month ago. I see I need to shed some clothes to catch up with you.

"You better help me, Slocum," she said, turning her back so he could undo the pinafore over her blouse.

No way he could unhook those tiny buttons and hold up the blanket too. He tied it as best he could at the waist and undid one button, but when his cover threatened to drop off his hips, only a quick snatch saved it. He tried the next pearl closure one-handed and finally was forced to resort to using both hands, only to have the cloth fall to his feet. The cool room's air passed over his most private parts. Without cover he proceeded to unbutton her dress.

She gave a glance down at the blanket on the floor. "Didn't take you long to get ready."

He never answered her, he just peeled the pinafore off her and reached around to feel her firm breasts as he kissed her neck. In a moment she squirmed around and faced him, pressing her ripe body to his as the last vestiges of her clothing fell away in her eager pursuit of pleasure.

Without a word they rushed to the bed and quickly nested in the mattress's well, enjoying the sensations of their eager bodies entwined. Faye's long, soft hair flowed over them as she moved over Slocum with the expertise of a woman twice her age.

She rode him with the fury of a bronc peeler. Her face turned up, she swept her hair back, then flung it over him like a fishnet as she bent down for him to taste at her fountains. Her nipples turned hard as rocks, and she moaned and pressed for more each time she switched from one to the other.

Slocum sat his horse in the tall cedars and waited. Soon he heard the approaching buckboard and the drum of the team as they trotted on the hard tracks.

He reined up the dun when the woman came closer and maintained his hidden place as she passed without his hailing her. She belonged to another man—she'd once done him a great favor. She wasn't on the run like he was, she had respectability, probably children, even if she was married to a polygamist—Ogallala and that time was over. This was another day; he had no right to complicate her life.

He waited in the grove until the sound of the buckboard had faded, then he sent the dun westward. He still had the Abbot brothers to shake.

2

A mantle of snow fell from his shoulders as Slocum shifted the saddle to his other side. The steady fall of large flakes had begun at sunup. Disoriented by the storm, he had little idea where he was, except that he was headed south. His handmade boots did not keep the snow from seeping in around the soles as he slogged through the wet accumulation. The piñon and junipers that lined the dim wagon road looked like canvas tepees under their icy coating.

The night before, sometime after midnight, the dun horse had colicked on something he had eaten. The horse's pawing and unmistakable grunts of pain awakened him. Nothing that Slocum tried, neither walking the horse around nor the whiskey that he poured down him gave the animal any relief. The horse's suffering only grew worse by the hour. At dawn it was apparent to Slocum as the groaning gelding laid on the ground that he needed to be destroyed. A .44 bullet to the brain ended the animal's pain and left Slocum afoot somewhere south of the Utah line in the no-man's land north of the Colorado River gorge called the Arizona Strip.

He estimated he was at least a hundred miles from Lee's Ferry on the Colorado, the only place to ford the river for hundreds of miles. An old acquaintance of his, Captain John Lee, would fix him up with him a horse. Lee and his English wife, Emma, traded with the Navahos at his outpost. The Mormon commander, Slocum knew, also had several other wives in Utah, where they raised peaches and irrigated fields along the Colorado. Lee's place on the river was too far away for him to even consider walking all the way. There had to be some ranchers who lived on this land, and surely one of them would sell him a horse—all he had to do was find one of these individuals. His greatest fear in this snowstorm was that he might pass within yards of someone who could help him and not see him. Still he needed to keep moving.

He slugged on under the weight of his gear. The snow fell with greater intensity. Since no wind seemed to be driving it, he wondered if it would snow forever without a force to move the storm away.

Then he heard the distant tingle of bells above his footfall. He listened closely, but there was nothing, only the hush of the snowfall. Then far away a small clapper against metal resounded. The sound drew a smile on his lips and he headed faster down the road. Someone, something wearing a bell, was close at hand, and that meant folks—folks who would sell him a horse to ride.

He came into a large meadow and he saw the first snow-clad ewe raise her head, look up at him out of snowflake-blinded eyes, and bleat. He couldn't remember when a sheep looked or smelled or sounded any better to his ears. The herd grazed, undisturbed by the falling white flakes, their heads down as they moved, bleating and halting at times for the hungry lambs that dove into their mothers' flanks for warm milk.

He moved along the edge of the flock, eager to find the herder's wagon. Then through the curtain of flakes he spotted three horses standing hipshot beside a herder's wagon.

The sound of laughter grew louder as he neared it. The cries and protests of a woman drew a serious frown on his face as he narrowed his eyes. An upset-sounding woman shrieked in protest. He set his saddle on the ground, then undid the thong on the Colt's hammer. Her cries for help were coming from that camp wagon.

At his approach, a cowboy ducked his head outside to look around. He held a whiskey bottle in his hand. The shock written on the man's face at the sight of Slocum was enough for him to consider cover as the cowboy sought his own gun. No time to protest—Slocum reached the protection of a snow-coated juniper in a facedown dive as the shots rang out. Belly deep in the slush, he tried to see the shooter through the snow-weighted boughs of the evergreen.

"Boys, there's some sum bitch out here!"

"You shoot him?"

"Hell, I can't see shit in this snow. I aimed to, but now I can't see him nowhere."

"Arland! Get your pants up. We've got to get the hell out of here!"

"Hell, I ain't done with her yet!"

"We got to get to our horses before he starts shooting at us. Maybe Ned got him."

"Here's for you! You dumb sheep-screwing bastard!" one of them shouted, and fired several rounds in his direction as the threesome fled the trailer. The bullets ripped through the weblike foliage and branches above him. Snow fell in great sheets off the bullet-riddled tree as Slocum pulled down his hat to protect himself from the cold avalanche. He could hear them cussing him as they mounted up. Soon they were gone in a fury of hooves. He rose and checked around to be certain all of them had left.

The sheep herd had not stampeded far; he could hear them bleating again. But his attention was focused at the wide-open door of the camp wagon. No one else had emerged. Gun in hand, he hurried across the clearing. He noticed the dead collie lying under a fresh sheet of white, the red blood still fresh where bullets had smashed its brain.

"Anyone here?" he asked.

"Go away," someone sobbed inside.

"They've left," he said, waiting and wondering about the female voice.

"Go away! Leave me alone."

After a check to be certain there was no one else around, Slocum holstered his Colt. With caution he stuck his head inside the wagon and in the lamplight could see a naked figure huddled, sobbing, on the floor. For an instant, because of the short hair he thought it might be a young boy, but when he climbed inside, he could see by the features that it obviously was a woman. In her state of undress she would soon catch a death of cold. He swept her up in his arms and attempted to set her on the bed.

She began to beat him with her fists and cry out. "No! Not you too."

"Easy," he said, ducking his head to the side as he eased her onto the mattress. "You would have caught your death of cold on that floor."

"I don't care!" she wailed. "Get away from me, you bastard."

He turned away so as not to stare at her nudity, but her swift kick caught him in the back of the leg and spun him around. Defiance raged in her bloodshot eyes matted with tears—he saw her pear-shaped breasts with pointed nipples and the smooth curve of her hips as she tried to kick him again. Then in raging frustration she rose up and began to strike him on the upper arm and chest.

His situation looked impossible. He finally decided the answer to her unbridled anger was to bind her up in something to control her until her senses returned.

"What are you doing to me?" she screamed as he shoved her down on the bed. But too late she discovered that he had taken one of the blankets and bound her arms against her sides like a corpse with only her head sticking out.

"Lady, I'm not one of them," he said, out of breath and holding her prisoner.

"Who are you?" She narrowed her eyes to glare at him.

"My name's Slocum. Last night I lost my horse to colic and he died. I'm passing through. I need to buy a horse from you."

"You don't work for the WTS outfit?"

"No, ma'am."

She looked flustered in her confinement as she considered him. In relief, he could see reality returning to her features, and composure.

"You know what those three cowboys were doing to me when you came up?" She tried to twist and kick her way loose, but soon her attempt subsided.

"Yes, I think so," he said.

"They were taking turns raping me, mister!" A black mask of anger swept her tearstained face as she looked away.

"Ma'am, I'm sorry I arrived too late to help you." He never offered to loosen his hold on the blanket.

"Too late, way too late." She shook her head in defeat. "I guess you saved me from the youngest one. Both Arland Sikes and his cousin Ned had their turns. Damn, oh, damn. I suppose I should be grateful. Well, are you going to be next?"

"No, ma'am."

"It's rape old Matty day. Get on with it, cowboy, you've got me down."

"Matty? That's your name?"

"Yes. Matty McArthur."

"Matty. Slocum's mine. I'll turn you loose if you promise not to kick or hit me again."

"Hell, Slocum, I'd promise you damn near anything to be free."

He let go and rose to his feet, ducking beneath the wagon's low ceiling.

"I'll go outside while you dress," he said, eager to give her some space.

"Stay," she said, moving around behind him on top of the bed. "What's left to see? I'll be decent, I mean dressed, in a few minutes."

He looked out across the snow-covered meadow as the flakes continued to fall. He had planned to be in Prescott in four days. Without snow the journey would require three hard days riding to get there; with the snow fall it might require a week.

"You always by yourself out here?" he asked.

"Two weeks ago my father had a serious wagon accident. He's laid up at the ranch. Those damn cowboys that you ran off put wings on our herders' feet last month. So I have herder duty because we haven't been able to hire anyone. You aren't looking for work?" she asked, standing up and finishing buttoning her man's wool shirt.

"No, ma'am, all I need is to buy a horse and ride south."

"I can't believe this happened." She sat down on the edge of the bed. "I was fixing breakfast when they rode up—Lord, you don't want to hear about my problems."

He pulled up a keg to sit on and looked at her. "If it helps to talk about it, go ahead."

"Oh, I can't." Tears began well up behind her brown eyes. She turned and flopped facedown on the cot to cry some more.

He busied himself stoking up the fire in the small stove. He'd seen the Arbuckle coffee box, and thought how he could use a cup of coffee, and so could she when she recovered. The small heater was soon putting out warmth, and her muffled crying and shaking of her shoulders subsided. There was no more he could do to ease her pain.

She finally sat up, fluffed her short hair back, and dabbed at her tearstained face. Her eyes averted Slocum and she managed to stand up and move to the small dry sink.

"Guess coffee would be in order?" she asked.

"Fine, Matty. I can do it."

"No, you've done enough. I thought I was going to go mad before they left here. I might have, but I began to think there wasn't anyone to care for those sheep or for my father."

"As grim as it gets sometimes, life has to goes on," he agreed with a solemn nod. Seated with his knees apart, he studied the wagon's worn pine flooring.

"One day"—she snuffed—"you're a virgin, the next . . ."

At the sound of her voice fading, he whirled in time to catch her as she fell. In his arms she felt limp as a rag as he laid her on the cot. He looked down at her unconscious form and shook his head in sympathy. It was a damn shame he hadn't kicked those cowboys butts; they deserved more than was done to them.

Satisfied she would sleep off some of her pain, he finished crushing the aromatic beans in the grinder. With the water on to boil, he sat back and wondered about Matty McArthur. She was older than he had first thought, probably in her early twenties.

He found some sliced bacon set out on the dry sink, no doubt cut earlier, before her attackers arrived, and some peeled Irish potatoes. He put the cast iron skillet on the stovetop. He could eat even if she couldn't. Maybe when she finally awoke she'd have some appetite.

The bacon was sizzling when she rose, holding her head. In an instant her eyes flew open.

"I'm sorry, Slocum," she said. "I thought for a second that you were one of them."

"I understand, Do they have any law up here?" he asked.

"No, they have to come from Prescott when they do."

"You are going to file charges against them?"

"Charges! Are you crazy? Who'd believe me? My word against theirs."

"Rape is very serious business."

"In court, who'd believe a sheepherder's daughter?" She shook her head, then pushed her short hair back from her face. "The three of them would lie their tongues off. They'd go free and I'd be the laughingstock of the Strip."

"They're liable to do it again."

"Not to me! I'll sleep with a double-barrel."

"How about some food?" he asked, to change the subject. "Since I helped myself to yours."

"Smells good. The sheep!" She started to get up, then turned her head to listen. "Are the dogs with them?"

"I think so," he said to calm her, recalling the dead collie outside the wagon. "I can still hear the bells."

"Strange, I haven't heard the dogs. Fine, we'll go check on them after we eat."

"You sure I can't do that? Go check on the sheep and you rest awhile?" he asked, concerned about her condition.

"We'll see about that. But I guess they'll be all right until after we're through eating. Food sure smells good. I feel kind of funny talking to you about all this. I hardly know who you are, Slocum."

"Not much to know, I drift around a lot."

"Oh, you cook good." She held up a crisp piece of bacon. "Maybe I could hire you to cook for me."

"I better not take it. The job, that is."

She closed her eyes and bowed her head in defeat. "I sure never encouraged them to do that to me."

"You didn't have to. They were drinking, weren't they?"

"I did smell liquor on that Ned's breath. Oh, Slocum, promise me that you won't tell anyone about this?" Her large brown eyes pleaded with him.

"Why?"

"My father—he would try to kill those boys if he ever knew."

"You're worried about him?"

"Yes, I am. He's laid up right now, but he'd get out of

his deathbed to try and kill them if he ever knew what they'd done. I know he would, and that Texas WTS outfit is mean as snakes.'' She poked her fork in the air as if she were spearing those snakes. ''I'll get them. You wait and see.''

''I don't doubt it. How many dogs do you have up here?'' he asked, holding the warm enamel cup in his hand.

''Three, why?'' She blinked at him.

He reached over and closed his fingers on her forearm to comfort her. ''They shot a collie out in front.''

''Big Boy! Those bastards,'' she swore, but he restrained her from rushing outside.

''Nothing we can do for the dog. I'll go see if I can find the others.''

''Finish your coffee,'' she said, subdued. ''We can only hope the other dogs got away. I never heard them shoot him, but the way I was fighting and screaming, I couldn't hear anything.''

They went outside together. She wore a wide-brimmed hat and a long-tailed oilskin coat. Where the dog lay, she bowed down to look at the snow-covered form. She brushed away some of the accumulation to see his face, then rose and somberly nodded—it was Big Boy.

Her shrill whistle brought no response at first. Then two large black collie crosses came bounding over. They circled Slocum, barking, and bounced all around Matty.

''Good dogs,'' she bragged, and patted them. Then she made a sweeping motion with her arm, and as if on cue they ran off, barking, through the white curtain that reduced visibility to thirty steps.

''They'll bring the herd back,'' she said.

''Good, we just wait?''

''Wait is all.'' He studied the snow falling, and agreed. Even if she had a horse to spare, for the time being he'd be foolish to stumble off some mountain looking for his way to Lee's Ferry.

•   •   •   •

Rafter Sikes smoothed his handlebar mustache with the fingers of his right hand. That damn snow, he thought, it would cost him a couple hundred head of cattle. He looked out the open front door of the headquarters house. The stuff wasn't going to stop soon either.

"You born in a damn barn, or you just jackass enough to enjoy the cold?" Barbara Sikes demanded.

"Just wondering where those boys were at is all, mother," he said. His wife had the cuttingiest way with words of any woman in the world.

"Those dumb boys could have fell off into the Grand Canyon, no smarter than they are."

"You're a little hard on your own flesh and blood, aren't you there?" he asked, looking with a frown toward the kitchen.

"Them boys are Sikeses, they sure aren't any kin to me," his wife shouted from the other room.

"I recall you having two of them boys and thinking they was the cutest ones in the country when they were toddlers."

"Then you took them and they ain't been worth a plug of tobacco since."

He sat down in the rocker beside the fireplace. Barb, she talked tough, but two hours later she'd be worried sick about those boys of hers being out in a storm like this one.

If he could simply keep the stinking sheep off this range, he might be able to make a living running cows. He leaned his head back and savored the motion of the chair. That Scotsman McArthur was like a sand burr, that damn tomboy girl of his, Matty, was worse.

The Navahos, they knew better than to come past House Rock Valley with their flocks. And he and the boys had even convinced two of those big outfits that enough was enough, and they turned around and drove their herds clear off of the Strip. Why, they left right after he and the boys tied tin cans to their herders' burros' tails. McArthur was a different story. The damn stubborn Scot brought his sheep up on the Kiabab plateau like he owned the place.

Damn snow kept stacking up outside, he'd have to range up into Utah to steal enough stock to cover his winter losses. Another problem keeping him awake at night were the Mormons who kept slipping in and taking out homesteads in those watered valleys in the northern part of the Strip. They were good places for his cattle to get out of the winter wind and most had open water the year round for stock to drink out of. Worse than fencing his stock out, he simply hated those pious Mormon farmers crowding onto his land.

"Them boys probably found them a cabin to hole up in," Barbara said, wiping the flour from her hands onto a sack towel as she came into the living room.

"Probably," he said, rising up from his seat to toss a juniper log on the fire.

He watched her go back in the kitchen. Barbara Sikes stood five six, thin as a buggy whip in her button-up-the-front calico dress. Her silver hair was pulled so tight into a bun that it gave her green eyes a slight slant, but they missed few details. She'd long ago given up sleeping with him. Besides, she'd told him, a man past fifty didn't need to be rutting her around. Did no good anyway, she was as barren as any old cow and had been for ten years or longer.

He was grateful she didn't know about the buxom young widow Naoma Worthen up in Dry Creek. What Barbara didn't know didn't hurt her. He resumed rocking. The chair clacked on the floor as he used his head to propel himself back and forth.

"I'm going to feed the saddle stock," he finally announced.

"Don't fall down out there!" she shouted after him.

Fall down? She think he was some tottering old fool? Naoma Worthen had some nice things to say about him. Never mind, someday Barbara would die and he'd move the widow down and they'd sleep together on her mattress. He'd show her, she could look down from heaven or up from hell and see him piling on Naoma in her bed. *Don't fall down!* She had her nerve. He buttoned up the jumper and slammed on his hat.

The weather outside wasn't as cold as he'd expected. Big wet flakes, probably snow for a week at this rate, and then starve half his cows to death. He had enough trouble with the sheep moving in. He hadn't come all the way from Texas to be rooted out by some damned old stinking sheepherders.

Inside the barn he poured the sweet-smelling barley from the sack into some canvas pails, then carried them out in the lot among the kicking and squealing saddle horses, making small piles for them to individually eat at.

Despite his scolding, the horses ignored him and they ran about, arguing over the grain and whirling to kick one another. He finally gave up on stopping their quarreling. Perhaps next week it would thaw, melt this mess and he would get a chance to go see Naoma.

He doubted the boys were coming back that night. Maybe they'd run McArthur's sheep off a bluff—he'd sent them over to scout the herd. They'd scared the piss out of the two boys that McArthur had herding the sheep. They'd left like jackrabbits after the boys shot up their camp.

Word was out up at Joseph's Lake that McArthur had had a bad wreck in his buggy. The accident couldn't have been more fortunate for them. With him laid up, only that smart-mouthed Matty was left to tend the sheep. Maybe his boys had put enough of the fear of God in her, enough to make her want to leave.

He looked up as they rode inside the barn alleyway. Snow-covered mummies, they dismounted heavily without a word.

"Kind of cutting it close, coming back in this kind of weather?" he asked.

No answer, they just shook their heads as they unsaddled their mounts.

"What did you boys do today?" he asked, feeling a little concern at their silence.

"Tell him, Arland," Steve said.

"Yes, tell me." Rafter listened close; something wasn't right about them since they'd returned.

"We got Barney McKey at the store to promise to stop selling them McArthurs anything on credit."

"He going to do that?"

"Damn right he is. I told him every cattleman in the country would stop trading with him if he didn't. How's that?"

"Sounds good. What else?" He knew they had done something else and were holding back telling him. They weren't fooling him: He knew those three boys like the back of his hand.

"Well, we intended to teach that tomboy a thing or two," Arland said, not looking up as he stood, holding the saddle in his arms.

"And?" Rafter frowned at the three of them.

"Well," Arland finally said with a shrug, "we got carried away and stripped off her clothes and then, well—we raped her."

"All three of you?"

"No, I never got to," Steven, who had turned sixteen that spring, said. "Because Arland was taking too long with her and then this dude rode up."

"Who rode up? Can she say in court that you two boys raped her? Can this guy be a witness?" He held his temples in disbelief at their blundering ignorance. Already he could visualize the sheriff riding up and arresting the three of them.

"Paw, quit making such an issue out of it," Arland said. "We raped her and that'll teach her that she can't mess with us Sikeses."

"And you boys can go do a couple of years in Yuma Prison."

"I ain't doing no time for nothing," Arland said. "Not for her or another like her."

"You boys better head out for the line camp on Wolf Tongue. I'll bring some supplies up there to you." He wondered how long they would need to hide out until this matter passed over. A good lawyer in Prescott could get the warrants withdrawn—might cost him several hundred, but he'd pay it.

"Paw, in this weather she can't get to the sheriff in Prescott for days," Arland said with a weary shake of his head.

"Guess you're right. Who rode up on you?"

"We ain't sure," Ned said, "but I may have gunned him down. He never shot once after I shot at him and we rode out."

"Murder, rape, what else they going to charge you three with?"

"Hell, we was only having a little fun. Boy, I'm here to tell you that hellcat squalled like a stuck hog when old Ned put his in her the first time." Arland laughed out loud.

"Damn boys, this is serious business." He was trying to think how to keep them out of the grasp of the law. "You don't mention a single word about this to your mother, and tomorrow you three head out like I said to the line shack. I'll bring you supplies and you keep low until we see what they're going to do about it."

"Paw," Arland said, draping an arm over his shoulder as they headed for the house. "This will all blow over."

"We'll see, son. We'll see." He wondered about their safety as they pushed toward the headquarters in the ever-deepening snow.

3

"We've got some hay at our place near Joseph's Lake. We better move the sheep down there," Matty said, sweeping thick flakes from her lashes.

"Unless you have some instinct about weather, we might wait until tomorrow and let this storm pass on through," Slocum said, concerned that they stood a good chance of becoming lost in the maddening snowfall.

"Will it be over by then?" she asked, the layer of flakes already covering her dark hat.

He shook his head without a good answer for her. "Might, might not, but there's no sense taking a chance."

"I suppose you're right. I think we're about a day's drive from our place if it doesn't get too deep for the sheep to drive through."

"We may have to beat out a trail. How much hay have you got?"

"A couple weeks supply is all. We were going to take them down to House Rock Valley for the winter. They say it stays open better down there. I was going to have them moved, but the herders ran off and my father had his accident."

27

"I don't know much about this weather. I've been through this country at other times of the year, but this snow is something else."

"They had an open winter last year. We spoke to some of the Mormons and they said the snow lasted only a few days, then it melted each time."

"How far is the drive to House Rock?" he asked.

"Thirty miles or so."

He shook his head. Before this was over, he suspected, they would wish the herd were in the valley and off this mountaintop. He dug out a quirlie from his vest inside his canvas coat, struck a lucifer with his thumbnail, and drew deep. The warm smoke he inhaled swirled in his lungs and settled him as he watched her wade after the dogs that bounced around the tightly packed herd.

As he savored the smoke, he recalled setting down his saddle earlier. He decided he better go find his rig and put it up before it was buried too deep to locate. In the fluffy accumulation he finally managed to locate it by kicking around with his boot toe. The snowfall was coming down at the rate of several inches an hour now.

He packed it to the wagon and stowed it on the tongue. She came back from the herd.

"They'll be fine. The dogs have them settled down and I think the snow has them flustered enough to stay until morning."

"Something on your mind?" he asked.

"I need to go check on my father," she said.

"What do you have to ride?"

"I have my horse, Strawberry. He can find his way home blindfolded. He's tied up with the two burros out back of the wagon." She tossed her head in their direction.

"What do you want me to do?"

"Keep an eye on things while I'm gone. If you don't mind? And I'll bring a saddle horse back for you in the morning."

"Fine, I'll pay you for it."

She looked at him as if there were something else she wanted to say, instead, she simply nodded to acknowledge his reply and then went for her horse. He watched her disappear. He stuck his head in the wagon and searched for her saddle and pad. They were piled in the corner, so he climbed in and secured them.

"You know choosing sides with sheep folks can be unhealthy," she said, placing the pad on the horse's back.

"Truth was known, I live unhealthy most of the time."

"I can't figure," she grunted, hoisting the saddle in place after refusing his help. "Why, you'd even stop for a sheep wagon from the looks of your clothes."

"I was afoot, but I'd stopped anyway."

She looked at him for a moment, then nodded. "I think you're shooting square with me." A tight set to her jaw and she girted up the gelding. "I just can't figure how you got this far off track."

"Just drifting through," he said, and stepped in to hold the horse's head for her to mount up. She didn't need to know about the Abbot brothers, who were trying to fill a bounty poster with his name and face on it. He hoped his false trails had worked out and they were headed for Salt Lake City by this time. Lyle and Dirk Abbot were two hardcases he would sooner or later have to settle with. For the time being they should be ranging northward and he headed south.

"I'll be back by early morning," she said. "We'll see how deep the snow is—I mean, I'll have your horse here by then, I was sort of wondering if you'd help me drive them to the hay yard."

"I can probably do that."

She forced a small smile of relief. "Thanks, Slocum. I'd better ride. Help yourself to the food."

"Thanks. You won't get lost in this blizzard?"

"I won't. Strawberry knows the way."

He waved good-bye and went back into the wagon for what was left in the coffeepot. He was still several days ride from Lee's Ferry. This snow had to be hurting anyone in pursuit of him as well.

From inside the wagon he could still hear the bleating of the herd and the bells. He finished the coffee, then stretched out on the cot and began to recall Evangeline, Evangeline Jordan. Her soft, sumptuous body and the good times they had shared at her Colorado ranch—damn those bounty hunters anyway.

He was about to fall asleep, when he heard a horse snort outside. His gun in his hand, he bounced off the cot.

"Hello, the wagon!" someone shouted.

No telling who it was; he did not recognize the voice. Carefully he pushed open the top half of the dutch door and tried to see who was out there. He held the six-gun against his leg, just in case.

"I'm looking for Wilson McArthur."

Slocum frowned at the obvious easterner standing and holding his horse's reins in the snowflakes. Who in the hell was he?

Rafter Sikes sat at the head of the table, ready to eat supper. The less she knew about their business the better it would be, he thought. He needed to think of something to take them away from the ranch.

"The boys and I are going up to start gathering for a drive down into House Rock," Rafter Sikes announced later at supper.

Barbara blinked her eyes, a steaming bowl in each hand as she approached the table. "Kinda late, ain't it?"

"This early snow won't last," he said, and filled his plate with rice and gravy from the bowls she held in her hands for him.

"Don't kid yourself. The cows will starve before you get them off this mountain."

"No, they won't," he said, spearing a fried steak from the stack on the platter in the center of the table.

She took the bowls to each of the boys and let them ladle

out their own portions. Then she set the dishes on the table and went back for the coffeepot.

"Ma, why are you so sure that we can't get those cows off this mountain?" Arland asked.

"Hell, this bunch ain't done a thing right in a year. The four of you were going to buy some hay for the horses months ago. You never did that, and now it's too late to go after it."

"We've had problems."

"I say you four are so damned obsessed by the notion of one old man and a pipsqueak of a girl and a couple hundred sheep that you can't get one thing done right for yourselves."

"That's not it!"

"Then, Rafter Sikes, you tell me what is right! You've waited too late to sell cattle this fall. They'll be too thin to sell after this snow."

"We've got to protect the sanctity of this range, woman."

"And starve to death being so damn bullheaded." She shook her head in disgust and took the pot back into the kitchen.

"They won't be here long," Arland said out loud.

Rafter waved his fork to silence his eldest and looked toward the kitchen to be certain she had not overheard his boasting. She didn't need to know what they'd done to that girl. Besides, she'd say that he put them up to raping her anyway. He sure didn't need to hear those accusations for the next six months. Landsakes, that woman could get off on tirades that made him mad enough to want to strangle her.

They finished the meal in silence. After supper Rafter took his seat in the heavy rocker. Ned played the mouth harp. Rafter wished his late brother's son, whom he and Barbara had raised, knew another tune besides "Oh, Susanna." The boys finally turned in with a "good night" and went out to the bunkhouse to play cards, an activity their mother deplored, but in the sanctity of their place she remained silent.

Rafter kept rocking. She mended the gray dress in her lap. The eyeglasses they'd bought in Cedar City for her helped, because she didn't grumble as much doing close work as she had before.

"What are you going to do for money this winter?" she finally asked, looking over the spectacles on her nose.

"I've got credit. Besides, the cattle prices will be better in the spring." He kept rocking.

"I certainly hope so."

"They will be," he said, more to get her to shut up than he actually knew about the condition of the market.

"So you plan to sell in the spring instead of the fall and make more money?"

"Exactly." He rocked a little harder. This had not been his choice of days; those boys of his could face some serious charges over raping that girl, maybe more serious than he could buy them out of. His wife was right, they had no ready surplus of money without the fall cattle sale, but he'd put it off, not expecting an October snow to seal them in like this.

He needed a plan to get rid of the McArthurs, and all his problems would be over. Then they could go on running their business like they had for the past seven years. *Get rid of the damn McArthurs!*

"My name's Tad Markum," the young man said. "I'm looking for work and they told me at Joseph's Lake that Mr. McArthur needed some help."

"Slocum's mine. You must have missed their place in the snowstorm," Slocum said, motioning for the fresh-faced youth in his mid-twenties to come inside.

"I was beginning to think no one lived up here."

He wore canvas riding pants, knee-high English riding boots, and an expensive plaid woolen coat. The felt hat he removed was in the eastern style with a turned-down brim.

"Easy enough to do in this bad a snowstorm. What brings you to Arizona?" He indicated a nail keg for a chair for his visitor.

"Oh, you can tell I'm from back east."

"Yes, it is obvious. And what's a young man like you wanting to herd sheep for?"

"Last spring I completed my studies at Yale and decided I needed to get out and work the land, so to speak."

"Herd sheep?" Slocum eyed the man with apprehension—a Yale man wanted to chouse sheep around.

"That too, sir."

"Why? You could get an important job in some company back east. Never ever miss a hot meal." Slocum could still not fathom the youth's thinking.

"Have you ever worked in an office?"

He shook his head, no, in reply.

"Then you have no idea of the confinement. It is not different from a prison. Do you understand?"

"I savvy jailhouses," Slocum agreed, never having related the two before. "But this sheepherding can be tough business. There are some cattle folks up here who think all of them should be ran off into the Grand Canyon. And they may even try to do it."

"What about the law?" Markum looked aghast at such a notion.

"Hundreds of miles away. In places like the Strip, only the tough survive."

"Ah, but obviously there are some higher authorities who can change this situation."

"One," Slocum said, and placed his .44 on the tabletop between them.

Markum folded his arms over his chest and looked at the handgun. "I was quite proficient with a Remington target rifle in college. Your revolver is not the most accurate in the list of armaments available today."

"No, but it packs enough lead to keep down whoever

you hit with it. Most wars in this country are fought in close range.''

"At the drop of a hat, I suppose?''

"Exactly.''

"Well, I have received a lot of chiding since I arrived in the West. However, Mr. Slocum—''

"Slocum's fine.''

"Good, then I will learn how to live in Rome.''

"Rome?'' Slocum asked at the risk of sounding stupid.

"Oh, yes, there's a saying that when you are in Rome, you do as the Romans do.''

"Not a bad idea. You have a handgun, I take it?''

"Yes, in my saddlebags.'' The young man looked ready to do whatever Slocum told him to do.

Slocum was unsure if the dude was better off left unarmed than he was armed. The man's life might be in his hands either way.

"What model?'' he finally asked.

"A Smith and Wesson, .38 caliber.''

"We'll look at it after a while,'' Slocum said. "It's time to fix supper.''

"May I go outside and view the sheep?''

"Certainly, you know anything about them?''

"Nothing other than that they give wool.''

"Oh, yes,'' Slocum said, still not certain this young man could ever survive the Strip. "Go have a look. Then unsaddle your horse and give him some grain out of the side box. I saw some feed bags. I should have supper fixed by then.''

"How long have you been employed by the Mc-Arthurs?''

"Four hours.''

"Oh, I see. You're new here too.''

"Right,'' Slocum agreed. "I'm new too.''

4

They had breakfast in the camp wagon. Tad Markum had heated water to shave his tanned face. Slocum wondered how long that daily business would last with him out west. Shavings could be accumulated and done twice a week, but he said nothing to the man.

"Who are these menaces to the sheep business?"

"I think she named them as Texans, WTS brand or something like that."

"You mentioned *she* several times?"

"Matty McArthur, she'll be along this morning. Since her father had a serious buggy wreck, she's been in charge of the flock and everything."

"No other employees besides you?"

"I simply lost my horse and stumbled in here. Three cowboys had her treed when I arrived."

"Treed?" he asked with a frown.

"Oh, it means trapped or surrounded." Slocum didn't want to explain how hounds ran varmints up trees and bayed them for the hunters. Why, he could spend a week talking and not have Tad up on all the things that happened out west.

"Did they do her any harm?"

Slocum shook his head to dismiss his concern. Matty wanted it that way—otherwise she could tell him. "They took a potshot or two at me and rode off."

"My, they must be quite incorrigible to do that to a woman."

"Tad, take my word for it. They are tough with a complete disregard for any humanlike qualities."

"What will you do when they return? They will come back?"

"Meet them head-on. Gun for a gun."

"What about her?"

"You're going to get to meet her. I heard a horse coming, and the way the dogs are barking, it's her."

"You perceived from that barking, it is her?" he asked, looking hard at Slocum.

"Yes, I did. They have different-sounding barks for everything."

"I shall try to observe that better," he said, and opened the top half of the dutch door.

Slocum had been out earlier. It had stopped snowing before midnight. The overcast sky still looked like the belly of a gray Canada goose with some obvious orange streaks of the sun trying to come through.

Matty came bouncing up and gave the dude a questioning look, but she took his hand to shake when he introduced himself.

"Slocum, I've got you a good little horse," she said, coming into the trailer.

"Thanks. We've got breakfast ready for you," he said, noticing Tad had gone outside.

"Who's he?" she hissed.

"Your new herder?" he said, controlling the mirth he felt.

"Why, he's a total pilgrim." She made a pained face in disbelief.

"He's not stupid, and with a few lessons he might be the best hand you ever had."

She shook her head and filled her plate with fried potatoes and bacon. Then, as she took a seat, she gave him her nod of approval at his gesture to fill up her coffee cup.

"He's looking for work," he said.

"What's he done before?" Her small lips set in a distrustful smirk, she cut her eyes around, distrustful at him.

"Gone to Yale college."

"What does that mean he knows?"

"He wants to be in the outdoors." Slocum shrugged. "I need help, but I can't become a durned wet nurse to some dude all fall long."

"I really think he's all the help you have coming."

"Damn—here he comes," she whispered.

Matty washed and dried the dishes; Slocum hitched the two large spotted donkeys to the wagon. Tad assisted him, observing each step.

"These, you say, aren't mules?" he finally asked.

"Not mules, simply donkeys, asses like in the Bible. A mule is horse-donkey cross."

"Hard to tell them apart."

"It is, because they all look alike at first. A hinny is a donkey–stud horse cross, and a mule vice versa."

"Are there many variations out here to look at?"

"Several."

"I shall study these, and when I see the different ones perhaps I can determine their varied ancestry."

Slocum simply agreed.

"What does she wish me to do?"

"Someone has to drive the wagon. Someone has to walk at the rear of the herd."

"I believe I shall take the walkalong job."

"Very good." Slocum did not relish either place, but considered driving the team as the lesser of two evils.

Matty soon came from the trailer and joined them, ready to start moving the herd.

"Slocum, you take the wagon south, you can read my tracks. The two of us and the dogs will bring the flock."

"The sheep should make it. The snow is melting."

"I think so."

"How is your father?" he asked, recalling she had said nothing about him.

"I'm concerned, but there ain't a thing I can do." She looked down at the packed snow.

"He's worse?"

"Yes, Slocum. I don't know what I'll do about him either."

"Perhaps we better take him to a doctor. Who's looking after him?"

"A neighbor lady, Mrs. Gray. He wouldn't hear of going to the doctor with the flock up here on the mountain."

Slocum looked off to the snow-coated junipers, small showers of tiny flakes drifting from the limbs. She had problems enough for two people. Tad was working with the dogs and looked very natural waving his arms to redirect some errant lamb. He shrugged; dude or not, he was a body, and they were short on them.

The Sikes boys had loaded two packhorses with supplies and bedrolls. Rafter felt as nervous as a longtailed cat in a roomful of rockers. Any minute he half expected some Coconino County lawmen to ride up in the wet snow and demand that his boys surrender. Maybe Arland was right, they couldn't get to Prescott for weeks in weather like this, and by then they'd be hid out.

"I'll be back tomorrow night," he told his wife, who stood on the porch without a coat and hugged herself for warmth. "We have trouble, I'll be home the next night."

"You all be careful and don't fall down and break a damn leg in this stuff," she said.

Did she think they were clumsy or something? He fussed

to himself until the boys finally were all mounted and they were headed northwest. Once he looked back before they rode into the timber; stupid old woman was still on the porch, staring after them.

"You think she knows about what we done yesterday to that Matty girl?" Steve asked, riding in close to his paw.

"God forbid that she ever finds out."

"She knows lots of things."

"We going to move cattle or stampede them sheep?" Arland finally asked.

"We better move cows or we won't have nothing but bones to sell next spring."

He tried to pick the best way to divide his forces so he could get to go up to Dry Creek and see her—the widow woman.

"Ned, you and Arland scout the Deer Lick country and force all those cows east. Steve and I will work north. By dark tonight everyone be at the Wolf Tongue line shack."

By midmorning he had his youngest son working cows out of the breaks and he was trotting his pony toward the widow's. He rubbed his palms on his pants leg a dozen times as his stomach churned in anticipation of seeing her again. Why, it had been two weeks—maybe three—since they'd tousled in her bed. This roundup business was the best idea he'd had in three years. Scattering the boys out worked perfectly for his plans.

Maybe she knew something about McArthur's wreck and his condition. Suit him fine if the Scot was unable to ever herd again. They would quit sooner that way.

He rode along, thinking about Naoma's short, chubby legs that looked like German sausages, the swell of her small belly—simply thinking about it raised his heartbeat as he rode along. By damn, he had the perfect plan and had all day to spend with her before he had to ride up to the line shack and meet the boys.

When he rode off the rimrock on the narrow trail, he was so intent on her, he never considered the wet snow under his pony's feet. When the bay slipped and tossed him hard to the side, he grasped the horn in a last pitched attempt to save himself from going off the edge. But his weight only pulled the animal down more as it scrambled for its footing on the slushy ledge.

All Rafter could see when he glanced down were the cornstalk bundles far below. Then he began to lose his grip on the horn. Unable to get his feet under himself, he and the snorting horse went off the bluff.

He landed on his back, bounced twice, and only the deep snow prevented a harder landing. The air driven out of him, he gasped desperately as his body slithered out of control down the steep cliff face like a runaway bobsled. In desperation he tried to grasp needled branches, but they ripped his palm causing him deep pain. Nonstop, he knew little in the blur of his falling and tumbling until he finally slammed against a stunted juniper trunk and the ache in his ribs felt like a dozen hot spears jabbed into his side.

He regained his consciousness to discover his legs were dangling over another thousand-foot drop. There was no sign of his horse. It had no doubt gone to the bottom and a pained death. He was uncertain why he was still alive, and blacked out again.

He awoke in the bright sunshine. The cold wetness from the melting snow had seeped into his clothing and made him shiver. His legs felt like they had been severed from his body. He dared not move, having discovered half his body hung over the lip of the precipice with nothing but an awesome chasm below. Grateful for the gnarled trunk of the juniper, he clung to it as he searched around for a way out.

Maybe he could walk . . . He drew up his right leg, searching with his knee for something solid. Small chunks of rock dislodged by his actions fell, clinking when they struck ledges below and then plunged farther.

His knee finally on the rock, he drew himself uphill until his entire body was resting on the steep shelf rock. His heart raging, ragged breath scouring his throat, he rested on his side, still uncertain of his ability to walk.

In the wreck he'd lost his Colt. The holster was empty, but that seemed insignificant as he painfully rose on all fours on the abrupt face of the mountain. He inched forward on his hands and knees where ledges stopped his descent off the cliff. After he'd crawled almost a half hour in snaillike fashion, he discovered a sheer face to the mountain, and crept backward to search for a new way. Every few seconds he peered off, seeing brown cones in the white fields far down the canyon. She could never hear his shouts, so he saved his breath for the effort he put forth to escape the mountain.

Barbara would say it was his punishment from God for being involved with another woman. But she wouldn't have him in her bed. What was a man suppose to do? Besides, his wife was no saint herself. The way he figured it, she'd once slept with a cowboy Turk Johnson. She never admitted it and she never denied it either. That had been years before, Johnson had been a smooth bugger who come down the road when they lived in Texas.

If it hadn't been for the fact that their boys were little then, he figured she'd have left with Johnson. She wasn't taking them boys of his. That might have changed her mind.

He held his left arm closer to his side. He had some broken ribs; he knew that pain. Damn, Naoma, can't you see I'm up here in a helluva fix? He collapsed in the melting snow and tried to squeeze the hurt out of his throbbing head.

5

"Give me the rifle," she said, riding up on her short roan.

"What for? Have we got bad company?" Slocum asked from inside the wagon.

"A mountain lion's been tracking us all day."

"Big one?"

"Good size, guess he figures a sheep will be easier to kill than a mule deer in this slush."

"You've seen him?"

"I've caught a shadow of him a couple of times."

"How's Tad working out?"

She looked back to be certain he wasn't in hearing range and gave Slocum a peeved look.

"He asks too damn many questions."

"He's a degree man."

"Hell, I ain't the West's best source of information either." She shook her head ruefully, took the Winchester, and turned her horse away.

"Need help to kill this cat, come get me."

"I can kill a lion," she said.

"Be careful," he shouted after her.

He clucked to the donkeys and they hit their collars. Not real swift draft animals, but easy to keep on grass alone when they were out on the range and gentle enough for anyone to use to move the camp wagon every few days.

An hour later he heard the report of the rifle as the shot reverberated across the black sage meadow. The cat had obviously gotten bolder and came into her sights. In a short while some unmistakable pistol shots sounded over the constant bleating of the flock and their bells, and he kept driving onward.

Out of breath, Matty finally rode up and Slocum reined in the donkeys. She handed him back the rifle.

"Well, that dude ain't a half-bad shot. I downed it, but he finished it off with his pistol. Big cat, I'll show you tonight, we're saving the skinning until we get to the ranch."

"I told you he would be good help—"

A scowl of disapproval on her face, she pointed her finger like a gun at him. "You don't have to answer all his damn questions. Just drive the wagon, Slocum."

"This snow has sure melted today," he said.

"It has. I think we can move the flock to House Rock tomorrow after we feed them good." The smile on her tanned face warmed Slocum, though he was eager to escape the confinement of the sheep wagon.

He meant to mention to Matty that most lions traveled in pairs and the other one might be close by. Sun out and all, they shouldn't have any problem seeing another slink up on the flock. He settled into his chair and flicked the donkeys with the lines—boring occupation, moving a camp wagon. All he could see as the wagon swayed along was out the front door and what was ahead of them.

They arrived at the McArthur headquarters in midafternoon. Matty had gone to the house to see about her father. Slocum unhitched the mules with Tad's help.

"What do you think about sheepherding?" he asked the young man.

"The scenery, I guess, is the best. The sheep, I can see, get to be very individual, you know?"

"Oh, yes," Slocum agreed, and carried out his harness to put on the wagon tongue. Individual—he wasn't staying there long enough to find that out for sure.

She came back swishing her riding quirt alongside her legs in the divided skirt. Slocum looked for some sign from her about the man's condition.

"He wants to meet both of you," she said.

"How is he?" he asked.

"Same," she said with a shrug.

"What did the doctor say?" Tad asked, brushing off his palms, as he was finished with his portion of the unharnessing.

"There hasn't been a doctor. There isn't one up here," Slocum said.

"You mean no medication, no physician—"

"Right, none of that," she said quickly. "Some freighters found him along the road under the overturned buckboard, brought him to Joseph's Lake."

Tad looked at Slocum incredulous. Slocum shrugged, he had no answer, that's the way it was. They both started for the house after her.

"Oh, Mrs. Gray is taking care of him," Matty said over her shoulder, "while I'm herding sheep. She's a neighbor lady."

"We'll skin that cat later," Slocum told Tad as they reached the doorway to the log cabin.

"Good, I've never done that," Tad said, and removed his hat when he entered.

"I'll teach you how to do it."

"I really am excited about that puma."

Both men drew up to the bed and saw the milk-white face under the gray beard on the pillow. Wilson McArthur had once been a big, robust man, Slocum felt certain.

"Howdy, men." His words came from a dry throat. Still

on his back and not offering to rise, he held up his hand
to shake with them.

"Sure pleased you two lads are helping me girl. I should
never have come"—his speech was broken by his deep
coughing—"I expect in time this whole range will be covered with sheep. Just tough being the very first one."

Slocum shook the man's hand after Tad. He gave him a
firm nod too and stepped back.

"You're Slocum? She said you ran them Texans off.
Shame you didn't kill them. Harassing a girl like that. I'd
beat in their heads if I'd been there. But I appreciate you
doing what you did, lad."

"Nothing." Slocum dismissed his concern. The man
knew only that they had come to scare her off—he had
enough troubles in his present condition without worrying
about Matty.

"You need your rest, Father," Matty said, and kissed
him on the forehead. As the three of them started to leave,
Mrs. Gray replaced the disturbed covers and said something
to McArthur that Slocum couldn't hear.

"There's hay to pitch. They need feed, they've eaten this
place around here clean this year." Matty tossed her head
toward the pens.

"Sheep to feed." Slocum laughed. "And a slave driver
of a boss."

"What do you think about him?" she asked, looking
serious again.

"I'm no doctor, Matty. I can see he's not the kind of
man who lies in bed. Must be broken up inside. Can he use
his feet?"

"Not much." She shook her head and then bit on her
lower lip. "That's what worries me the most. I'll go get
those pitchforks and meet you two down there at the gate."

Tad trailed along as Slocum headed for the haystacks.
Matty went to the barn to get the forks.

"Why is McArthur so dead set against doctors?" Tad
asked.

"Don't believe in them, I guess. There's lots of folks like that."

"Modern surgery has—"

"Wait, Tad. The doctors we've got out here aren't from those schools."

"Oh, I see."

They waited at the gate for Matty to come with the forks. All the sheep must have been bleating at once that they were hungry.

How in the hell would he ever get down? Rafter Sikes asked himself as he lay on his back in the small rivers of melting snow on the face of the mountain. Be a helluva note to die on the side of this cliff in plain sight of that woman's cabin, but there was no way up or down this ledge except to climb down one of the chimneylike crevasses in the mountain's face. He had been from one end to the other. With his broken ribs and the left arm so sore when he dared raise it, he wondered if exposing himself to such a hazard was smart or not.

Be careful and don't fall. That old woman had really gotten his gall up saying that. He had been careful, it was the damn horse that slipped and fell. Way past noon, sun time. If he was coming off, the crevice was the only route down. Using his feet and back to position himself between the rock walls, the climb down would probably take him all afternoon.

With a deep intake of breath and resolve, he bellied himself off into the narrow crevice in the face of the mountain, his boots dangling over a thousand or more feet of open air as he tried to get situated in the shaft. A search for a small ledge for his boot toe. The one he located did not hold half his weight, and when the toehold gave way, giving his empty stomach a jar, he managed to maintain a firm grasp on the rock outcropping.

At last he found a lip to hold and began easing himself back until he could use his body and legs as a brace to lower himself down the narrow corridor. He didn't dare look down; there was nothing under him to break his fall. Over a thousand-foot drop beneath him.

Inch by inch he released the pressure and worked his way down the shaft. His leg muscles ached, the pain shot through his chest when he applied pressure to his back to hold himself upright in the corridor.

What if the slot grew too wide, or even too narrow, to do this? Both were possible—he had studied several such passages. Maybe somewhere there was a ledge he could get out on. At the moment, one wide enough to stand up on would be wonderful. He eased himself down some more, already the spot above where he had climbed in looked too narrow.

His mouth too dry to swallow and the cramps in his legs more and more painful, he systematically lowered himself. Still higher than the floating buzzards in the canyon who were soaring over his dead horse, he tried to think why he was doing this—for her, of course. That sheepherder McArthur whom he hated so bad, he'd live to see him driven out of this land. His boys and the ranch—that was why. He'd not come out here from Texas to get overrun by sheep people. He'd come to build a great ranch for him and the boys.

He'd always dreamed, too, about having fancy folks at his big ranch house for social events. Like the governor or senators, as rich folks did back at home. No need to build a big house until Barbara died, she'd complain about it all the time. Naoma wouldn't. He could see her in a fancy dress, serving food on a tray to all those bigwigs. That girl had class. Barbara, on the other hand, came from Tennessee, pure hillbilly, no sense of society. Why, she'd wear some old dress she'd mended until you couldn't tell what color it was new and fit like a feed sack.

Out of breath, he paused, set his soles into the opposite wall, and cut the perspiration off his face with the side of his hand. Hot in this oven, he must be a long way down.

But a look over the side denied him that, and he quickly turned back to face the red sandstone walls. He still had a long way to go.

Inch by inch the sharp pains and cramps grew. His side of the mountain became shaded as the sun slipped westward. Cold soon replaced the sun's heat, and he wished for the jumper he'd left on top to lighten his load. The rockface behind his back was eating up the material in his vest and his back pants pockets.

He slumped in gratitude when his rump finally settled on a shelf large enough to sit on and he let his achy legs dangle. He could watch the shadow of the mountain lengthen across the valley below. The trip to the floor that should have taken only a half hour on horseback had been going on all day.

Full of dread, he resumed his downward movement. The resting had only teased his sore muscles; they cramped harder and harder. If he could ever get down on the ground.

Shadows began to fade and twilight showed on the top of the mountain. The valley turned to inky black; he still fought for his descent. Pressing one foot, then the other, hard enough to support himself and then rolling his back so he could control his downward motion, he found new places for his boots and he'd go down another few inches.

The stars came out. Deeper cold turned his sweat to ice. He could hardly control the shaking in his body and was forced time and again to stop and try to steady himself.

Then his right sole slipped from the wall. He knew next he would fall down the chimney after it. A scream slipped from his lips as he lost his hold and began to plunge downward into the black well.

6

Slocum took his bedroll and headed for the barn. The sheep were bedded down in the lots beyond the headquarters. Except for the occasional tinkle of a bell, all was quiet. A sky full of stars shone from one horizon to the other through the boughs of the pines as he walked toward the dark outline of the log structure. His back muscles were sore from feeding the flock, the richness of the cured alfalfa still in his nostrils.

He entered the inky hallway of the barn. He walked down the alleyway and planned to spread his roll out in a pile of hay beside the grain room.

The canvas sheet spread out and the blankets undone, he squatted on his boot heels in the alleyway, away from the hay, and enjoyed a last smoke of the day.

The cat they'd killed had been a tom. Big one, Slocum was surprised the horse that she'd brought up there for him to ride had let them load it and bring in the long carcass across his saddle. It seemed like a well-broken pony—the cat was dead, but he still must have smelled like a lion to the horse. Most horses had a strong dislike for the smell of a big cat either from experiencing an attack or by instinct.

Tad had worked hard to skin the big tom and together they'd nailed his hide to the shed wall. For one thing, the Yale man was a quick learner despite Matty's impatience with him. Maybe she would eventually get over some of her edginess: Her father's condition, besides the bitter incident at the camp, would stir up anyone.

He ground the glowing ashes out in the dry dirt, then moved over and sat on his bed roll to remove his boots for the first time in over a week. Even the night before he'd slept with them on atop the bunk in the camp wagon. Tad had chosen the wagon, but Slocum liked to sleep outside, varying the locations. Many times this plan saved bounty hunters slipping up on him.

Before he closed his eyes, he wondered where the Abbot brothers were sleeping that night. Some fancy hotel, no doubt. *Bastards.* He felt for the Colt under his saddle. Satisfied it was in place, he rolled over on his side and prepared to sleep, putting the knife in the scabbard near his hip.

The growl brought the hair straight up on his neck. Awakened by something in the barn, he had no idea the time. He could hear the soft, padded feet pace back and forth on the dirt of the alleyway. She was there in the barn. The female cougar had come looking for her mate—as he had wanted to warn Matty she would. He tried to see in the inky night, but all he could do was speculate in the blue darkness, and smelling her carrionlike odor, knew she was close.

He felt for his knife and drew it from the scabbard. She had smelled the male's scent on the saddle. The odor had attracted her to the barn. Slocum intended to give her the rig as a diversion, so he didn't reach under it for the handgun.

She was close enough that he could hear her breathing when he heaved the saddle at her and then came up with his knife. She snarled in alarm and her claws ripped at the leather in defense.

For a split second her white belly showed her location as she savagely fought the saddle. Time enough to distract her, he sprung for her back. One chance to sink his blade in her jugular vein, but if he missed, then all hell would break loose. He ripped across her throat with the keen-edged blade, slashing fur, windpipe, arteries, and muscle. The cat's protesting squall deafened him as she strained under him to twist from his grasp, then he felt the furious muscles melt and go limp as death took the big predator. Out of breath, spitting cat hair from his mouth, he managed to rise up, out of breath, and lean against a post.

"I heard it scream!" Tad shouted.

Slocum could see a lantern coming from the direction of the house. Matty's concerned voice was mixed with Tad's questions as they approached.

"Slocum! Oh, my God!" She held the lantern higher, then rushed to his side and supported him.

"Are you all right? Did it bite you? Where are you scratched?"

"I'm fine," he said, extracting more cat hairs from his mouth with his fingers. Yuck. "You have any whiskey?"

"Did you try to eat it?" she asked, growing amused at his discomfort and distaste.

"No."

"Is this the other one's mate?" Tad asked.

"She never said before she died," Slocum said, looking deep into Matty's brown eyes in the lantern light.

"I'll go find you that whiskey," she finally said as neither of them listened to the college man babble on about the significance of the second kill.

Rafter Sikes awoke when he heard the owl's soft hooting above him. He felt for broken bones. How long had he been out? Twice, in less than a day, he had fallen from a great height. This time no snow had cushioned his landing and he lay stiff, cold, his entire body shot with pain. On the loose, flat talus rocks worn from the mountain by time.

He closed his eyes and forced himself to roll over on all fours. After a pain-filled few minutes, he forced himself to a half stand. He saw the treetops beneath him so he must be near the bottom, he reasoned.

Stumbling, then catching himself, he worked his way down the pile of rocks to the soft ground at the base of the cliff. He used a juniper limb for support as he stood, swaying like a drunken man.

Damn, he must be a mile from her place. He charged off, limbs ripping at him as he staggered to his destination. Naoma would doctor him, she could fix him. She wouldn't have any whiskey—Mormon gal, but what the hell, just to have her hold him in her arms would be some solace. The whole damn day he had dreamed about her, her cradling his head in her lap, smoothing his face with her small hands until the cold chills ran up and down his arm.

He ran into a bough too tough to bulldoze through and it set him on his butt instead. Nothing could hold him back now, not man or beast. He had another quarter mile to go, maybe less. Winded, he gasped for air as he climbed the rail fence, spilled over onto his head, and sprawled out on the dirt. He was close, real close.

"Naoma! Naoma!" he cried, crossing the field of corn like a drunken sailor. The house stood dark. She must be asleep.

At the porch he fell facedown on the raw boards, unable to go another foot and again called her name.

"Naoma! It's me, old Rafter Sikes. Come out here, darling. I need you."

No answer.

He rose to his feet like a great wounded bear. His shoulder against the facing for support, he pulled the latch string and then shuffled into the house's black interior.

"Honey? It's me. Rafter."

No reply.

He fought to get a lucifer out of the fruit jar on the table and struck it alive, then held the flame to the candle. Where was she? There on the table was the note, in her fancy writing:

To my friends.

I have gone to Cedar City, Utah, to see my sister, Rachel Ames, and to help her with birthing her third child. There are jars of canned food in the cellar. Be sure to latch the door when you leave so the wild animals don't come in while I am absent the next month.

Naoma Worthen

The next month? He collapsed on the chair. Why, she'd probably come home and find him dead in her house. She never mentioned last time he visited her about her going to Utah. Maybe she had and he hadn't heard her, but gone for a whole month?

His head hurt and his side burned with pain as he buried his face in his arms and wept. His left foot had swelled so badly, he figured he would need to cut his boot off. And she was a hundred miles away in Utah—damn, his luck had turned sour.

7

They started before dawn to hitch the donkeys up and get ready to drive the sheep to House Rock Valley. Slocum and Tad had skinned the second cat the night before and tacked its hide to the other side of the shed to cure. Slocum could still taste cat hair, and spat occasionally while he hooked up the harness. He must have tried to bite the big cat. He finally decided all that hair amounted to some sort of revenge the cat was taking in return for her life. She should have stayed in the forests and feasted on the fat mule deer that were everywhere on the Kiabab.

Matty brought them coffee cups and a granite pot of the steaming brew as they finished loading down the wagon with supplies and food.

"We should make the drive in two days. Then I want to ride over to Lee's Ferry and hire some Navaho boys to stay with the herd. If I can talk the two of you into staying with the flock while I do all that."

"I think I'll be getting along good enough with the dogs by then," Tad said. "Slocum can go along and be certain that you're safe."

"I'm more worried about the Texans trying to do something to the flock," she said, dismissing his concern for her safety.

"I can handle a gun."

"Sure, but you haven't ever shot anyone. That makes a difference," Slocum said, seeing her point.

"Besides, if I can drive these sheep all over this strip by myself, I can certainly ride to the ferry and back unguarded."

"We'll guard the flock. You go hire some herders. Tad and I will remain with the flock."

"Good, let's get on the road. Slocum, would you stop at the store and get a sack of flour, baking powder, and some dried fruit," she asked.

"Cash or credit?"

"I have credit with Barney McKey. Have fun driving that wagon. I will bring Salty for you to ride once we make camp."

Slocum shook his head in defeat. Many more days driving the sheep wagon, and he might be ready to eat a sheep raw, wool and all. He stepped inside, lifted the reins, kicked off the brake pedal, and clucked to his donkeys. They came around and headed for the road.

They sold tobacco products at the Joseph's Lake store. A jack Mormon, this Barney McKey sold whiskey too— both legal and untaxed, according to Matty. All Slocum wanted was a handful of cigars to smoke in the evenings before bedtime or while driving donkeys.

Seated on the spring seat pinned on the floor behind the dutch door, Slocum kept driving, leaving the sheepherding to the other two. The road was muddy on top from the snow melt, causing the donkeys to sometimes stretch their necks in the harder pulls, but most times they went head-up and eased the rig along at a pace hardly faster than a snail's.

He had spoken with Matty's father some about his condition the night before, and the man complained that little of his body worked below his waist since the wreck. There was some movement, but Slocum feared he had all but given up ever being normal again and Slocum had no solution—except the girl needed him whole again. No way she could survive against the Sikeses and the cattlemen without some powerful help. Maybe he should convince her to give up this notion and sell out the flock.

He clicked to the mules and they trotted down the level road flanked by towering ponderosa pines. Perhaps the cattle interests would think they were leaving, moving the sheep to the valley. He hoped so for Matty's sake.

Later, inside the general store that smelled of saddle oil and pepper, Slocum knew several loafers were staring at him.

"Howdy, mister," the big man behind the counter said. His rolled-up sleeves revealed the red hair on his muscled forearms.

" 'Morning. I need a hundred pounds of flour—"

"Who's paying for this order?" the storekeeper asked.

"The McArthurs?"

"No." He shook his head. "They don't have credit here anymore."

The room became quiet as a pin. He noticed several of the store's population leaned forward to listen.

"I guess you didn't hear me," Slocum said. "I want one hundred pounds of white flour, two pounds of baking soda, and five pounds of dried apples."

"You don't smell too good to me," the big man said, spreading his hamlike hands on the counter.

"Smell ain't got a damn thing to do with it. When it comes to dying, that's when smell can be a real problem."

"Who are you, mister?"

"That ain't important. I intend to take four men with me to hell. Any of you want to sign up?" Slocum's hand went to his gun butt and several of the onlookers sucked in their breath as the Colt filled his fist faster than their eyes could follow.

"Any one of you want to die over a damn sack of flour, a tin of baking powder, and some dried apples, you better get out front here, otherwise I'll pick and choose who's going to die." Slocum surveyed the store loafers.

"You robbing me?"

"No, I'll pay cash for it. Keep those hands on the counter, I kinda like you that way. Old man, you go over there and you tote me a sack of flour out to the wagon."

Toothless, he rose from the chair, making a great effort to swallow something and then gave out a *baa*ing noise from deep in his throat as if he were dying.

"I swallered my tobaccy!" he finally cried, and looked sick enough to puke.

"Sit down, then," he ordered as the man began to cough violently.

"You there," he said to the huge man wearing a wool hat. "Take those items out to my wagon, please."

"I will," he said as he rose, showing he wore no firearm. "But I ain't taking sides in this war. I'll take them out for you, but I ain't choosing sides between cattle or sheep."

"Smart man. I'm sorry this came to such a confrontation." Slocum used his left hand to draw out a half dozen cigars from an open glass container. He held them up for the storekeeper to see and acknowledge, then stuffed them in his vest pocket.

"You know what, gunfighter," the storekeeper said, his hands still spread on the counter. "You've hired on the wrong side."

"Good, you know that boy you sent up to hire on with Mr. McArthur? That was fun too, wasn't it?" Slocum smiled and nodded as if considering the situation.

"That dude from back east. Called himself a Yale man?"

"That's the one. Only he's a federal agent and he has the goods on you about selling untaxed whiskey."

"What?"

"I'd say you might ought to shag out for Utah. Them

federal marshals get up here in a few weeks, you'll do some
hard time in San Quentin.''

"San Quentin?''

"How much do I owe you?'' Slocum asked, seeing the
positive side to his made-up threat.

"You're joking me about this federal man business?''
The man's ruddy complexion had faded to pale white and
the freckles on his face stood out like blood specks.

"Why joke when the truth is better? Three years ought
to be long enough. Tell me how much the bill is?''

"Two dollars, who cares.'' The man appeared in a daze.
He shook his head and blinked his eyes. "How long will
it take them to get here?''

"They should be here in ten days. You better get to
riding.'' Slocum slapped the Colt back in his holster.
"They tell me San Quentin is a bad island. I knew an
Apache chief was sent there for one year. Changed his
whole outlook.''

"What about a trial and all that?'' the man asked in a
high-pitched whine.

"You don't know? They never try whiskey tax evaders,
just sentence them is all they do for that crime. Gentle-
men,'' he said as he touched his hat and left the store.
Satisfied that he had the whole lot confused and concerned,
he whistled as he drove the wagon out to the road to meet
the flock.

"What's up?'' Matty asked, riding up and leaning on her
saddle horn.

"Your credit is no good back there.''

"What?'' She glared back with a frown at the distant
store.

"I have the goods. You can pay me.''

"I will, but why? We've always paid Barney on time.''

"Seems the cattle-sheep war is intensifying. Keep the
Yale man out of sight, I have them believing he's a federal
agent and they're all jail bound for making illegal whiskey.''

"You what?" She grinned and then shook her head in disbelief.

"Trust me, it worked. I may have scared your store owner out of town."

"Who got to Barney concerning our credit?"

"Who else but the Texas boys, huh?"

"Bastards." Her eye narrowed and her lips spread into a straight line.

"I know. Get those sheep moving. I'm headed down the mountain to make camp."

8

On the third day he hobbled over to the window to see his boys and several others ride up. Rafter managed with a homemade crutch to hobble out on the porch and survey them with a scowl. About time they got there, him eating her canned vegetables for all this time.

"Paw, you all right?" Steven asked.

"Do I look all right? It damn sure took you long enough to find me," he growled.

"We've looked every damn bit of this country over to find you," Sam Dugan said. An older rancher from west of Joseph's Lake, Dugan had interceded to defend his sons.

"Yeah," Cy Broyles added. "You never left no tracks when you took to flying."

His words brought some laughs, and everyone dismounted.

"How in the hell did you land down here?" Arland asked, looking around. "She at home?" he asked under his breath.

"Who?" Rafter asked under his breath.

"Naoma."

"Gone to Utah to help her sister with a baby, the note says."

"That's a shame," Arland said, and strode off.

Rafter looked at his son for a moment. Maybe he wasn't the only Sikes visiting the widow—they'd straighten that out when she returned.

"Paw, you need to get off that leg and tell us about this flight off the mountain you took. We found your dead horse about a half hour ago and I can't see how you got down alive," Steven said, guiding his father inside.

With his right leg propped up in a chair, he finished telling his story of the accident. The limb was still swollen and stiff. He suspected something was broken, but worse, he dreaded the thought of dragging it the rest of his life. Lots of ranchers and old cowboys were hobbled with such injuries. He hated to even think he would join the ranks of the disabled.

"They've moved the sheep off the Kiabab," Broyles said.

"But just to House Rock for the winter?"

"Maybe. We got word that McArthur ain't never got out of bed since that wreck."

"Too bad, ain't it," Rafter said, scrubbing his bearded face with his palm and considering his next move to eliminate the McArthurs forever.

"But before you think all you got to fight is a girl, tell him about that gunman in the store," Broyles said.

"I heard about them fast-draw guys," another interceded. "But this one is quicker than a cat can lick its butt, and this guy is armed. I never seen the like. Why, Roady Snell swallowed his tobacco, it was so damn fast."

"Boys, I don't give a damn what kinda gunmen they got hired. If we let them stay another season, there will be a million more head up here next summer." Rafter surveyed the others; they were looking undecided.

"That gunman said that tenderfoot was a federal man. He's with her too. If they sent a federal men in, we'll lose no matter what. Them stinking sheepherders have got more power in Washington than we little cowmen ever have.''

"Bluffing, is all," Rafter scoffed. "That's what he's doing. You want a couple million sheep up here next summer?"

"Hell, no!"

"Then I say we stampede their herd off a bluff and eliminate it. They didn't leave when we run off their herders. That was warning enough."

"I kinda hate it because she's a woman," Sam Dugan said, having serious reservations about the matter.

"Well, I hate sheep grubbing up every blade of grass on this plateau and all the rest of the country between here and the Utah line." Rafter's leg hurt and he squeezed the upper half with both hands as he waited to hear more.

"I'm with you," Cy said. "We've got to show them woolly bastards we mean business."

"Me too!" others began to pipe in.

Rafter looked directly at Sam. "You in or out? Ain't no being neutral in this deal."

"I seen one war, make it two, counting the big one. If we could be sure that no one got hurt—" Sam dropped his head and shook it with deep dread.

"You fought one war for what you believed in," Rafter said. "Was the second one about sheep?"

"No, it was over water. Boys, I hate sheep on this mountain worse than the plague. But we better be ready. There's going to be funerals, and they won't all be sheepherders'."

"My boys and I ran off those two big outfits that come out. No one was hurt." He looked at Sam and waited. He felt certain from then on it wouldn't be only the Sikeses fighting the sheep men, they would have numbers. Damn, that leg hurt—someone had to have some whiskey.

"I have to be with you," Sam finally surrendered. "But no bloodshed unless there is no other way."

"No bloodshed," Rafter agreed. No cattlemen blood anyway; he didn't give a damn about the others.

A cheer went up and then Steven pushed through with a bottle. He handed it to his father. "This should help that leg."

"A couple of gallons might." Then he lifted it to his mouth and swallowed deeply. The fire scorched his throat and warmed his ears in passage. The leg would be never-mind in a little while. For one thing, he had backing now and there would be no more sheep on the Kiabab.

"Let's cook something," someone shouted.

Rafter savored the small house alive with men after his three days alone. Men who were on his side. The pains from his fall would soon dissolve like the sheep problem and vanish forever.

Slocum whittled with his Barlow. He sat on the stope of the wagon and threw down the red shavings. Tad had the dogs well in hand and they were guarding the herd. He rode back from checking on them and dismounted.

"They act settled enough."

Slocum agreed as he surveyed the flock.

"You know that sheep are a preferred investment over cattle these days," Tad began, seated on the ground and hugging his knees.

"You taking up the business?" He looked mildly at the man for an answer.

"I may after I learn more. I plan to spend a year learning all I can about the business, then I may do that."

"If she'd listen to me, I'd tell her to pack up and leave."

"You think she will fail?" Tad frowned.

"No, but this sheep-cattle deal up here is about to fester like a bad boil. If it comes to a head, she has no one to side with her but the two of us. That's not good odds."

"I don't understand the way the law works out here. Isn't there any judicial force to stop this?" He held his arms out, including the whole country in his question.

Slocum shook his head and resumed his whittling. "No, there isn't."

"What will they do to her?"

He didn't want to tell him what had already happened to her. But that might be mild compared to what they'd try next to convince her to leave, since their cruel assault on her person had not changed a thing.

"Tad, it might be a good time for you to ride on. Find yourself a more peaceful place to tend sheep." He brushed the shavings off his lap as he rose, snapped the Barlow shut, and then looked off toward the bloodred Vermilion Cliffs that rimmed House Rock Valley.

"I am not afraid of a fight, Slocum. Granted I have never killed a man, but I have no great fear inside me concerning a life-or-death situation."

"Good. Then go to wearing that Smith and Wesson every hour of the day. I figure before this week is out, they will bring this damn war to us."

"You've seen this before?"

"Yes. Too many times—way too many times. It gets lots worse."

"She won't ever sell out and leave, will she?"

"No."

9

They struck in the night. Their gunshots and shouting awoke Slocum. From the distance he could make out the riders with their torches. Earlier he had spread his bedroll on the ground a hundred yards from the camp wagon. As he studied them, he could see by the starlight the large number of horsemen surrounding the wagon.

Too late, he grimaced, they had dragged Tad out and were roughing him up. As he slipped silently through the waist-deep arroyo, he regretted ever saying the man was a federal agent. From the words that he could hear, they thought they had captured a real one.

There were simply too many for him to rush in and try to save Tad. It would be better to hold off awhile. He might get both of them killed for his troubles. For the moment, nothing would rescue the young man from their hands. Later he might be able to free him. He felt between a rock and a hard place, unable to help the young man and mad as hell about the raid. Then several fateful gunshots reverberated across the sagebrush sea and the yelping of the injured dogs told him all he needed to know.

"You dirty bastards!" he heard Tad swear. "What do you want?"

Flames from the burning canvas top of the camp wagon began to lick the night. They might rough the young man up, but he doubted they were cold-blooded killers and that they would do anything worse.

He moved closer, Colt in hand.

"Take him along," someone shouted. They sounded divided about running him off and taking him captive.

Disappointed at the next turn of events, Slocum could see by the starlight when they put the hatless Tad on a horse. He also could recognize some faces in the light from the crackling fire of the camp wagon. He recognized them from the Joseph's Lake store.

"Some of you stampede those damn sheep!"

"Yeah!" came the cheer.

Even the barrage of gunshots into the air couldn't rouse the sleeping sheep to stampede. Unable to get them to flee en masse, the men began to shoot into the band. Pain-filled bleats, shots, and men cursing filled the night.

Slocum took a seat on the sandy wash. There was nothing he could do; nearly two dozen riders were out there now by his count. His stomach roiled at the violent destructive acts going on not a hundred yards away. He wanted to rise up and start killing them wholesale, but that would serve no purpose. Someone had to face Matty when she returned and found her dream shattered.

"Where's that fancy gunfighter?" someone shouted. "Did he tuck tail and run?"

"Look for him, boys," someone shouted.

Slocum rose up on his haunches, ready to fight. The Colt in his hand, they didn't want to find him. Not in the mood he was in. He waited.

Dawn painted the far rim of the canyon as they climbed the narrow wagon road. Rafter was tired; his right leg was swollen again and throbbed. The only satisfaction he had was that they had successfully raided McArthur's flock. That so-called government agent was their prisoner, and they must have shot a hundred sheep or more. He looked back over House Rock Valley. She'd give up after this. Her wagon burnt, her sheep dead, she had no other choice.

Where was that gunman and the girl? The gunman's disappearance niggled him. He pounded the saddle horn with his fist as the road grew steeper. They needed to find and eliminate him like they would this agent after they found out how much he knew. His horse rocked him so hard, cat-hopping up the steep hill, the pain down his right side doubled him over.

It'd be good to have this sheep deal over and done. He still needed to move a lot of his own stock down into the valley before it snowed again. A couple of bankers would be getting edgy, since he hadn't sold anything and paid on his notes. They could wait. He had more important things to do—eliminate those sheepherders, or there might not be any cow business at all.

"What we doing next?" Arland asked.

"Gathering cattle, pushing them down into House Rock, and you boys need to ride out in the morning and get busy doing that."

"What about him?" Arland asked, motioning toward Tad, who trailed along.

"Put him in the smoke house. Nothing in there. You lock him in good and I'll handle him later."

"He ain't very tough for an agent."

Rafter twisted with some discomfort. "May all be an act too." He turned forward as he drew the whiskey bottle from his saddlebags. It would take several good swallows to cure this much hurting.

Hours later at the ranch headquarters, Rafter eased himself from the saddle. She was on the porch, looking them over like some kind of judge.

"Who's he?"

"Federal man."

"My gawd, what did you bring him here for?" She looked aghast that they would dare do such a thing.

Rafter clung to the horn, descending slowly from his horse. The excruciating pain blinded him as he fought against unconsciousness. He wanted to kill Barb and shut her up as the chills of pain ran up his spine.

"To find out what the hell he knows," Arland shouted at her.

"I swear, you boys ain't a lick smarter than your stupid paw." At that, she stormed back inside the house.

"Get moving, dude," Arland said as he shoved the prisoner toward the stout log smoke house.

"You better tell them anything happens to me, they'll pay the price in federal court," Tad shouted.

"Shut up!" Arland ordered, and pushed him toward the open door. "There ain't no federal law up here."

"There will be!" Tad said in defiance as he was forced to duck and enter the log structure.

"Get in there," Arland ordered.

What in hell was a federal man doing up there anyway? Rafter wondered. His sweat-slick hands still grasped the saddle horn. His own damn government had even turned against him.

"Here, Paw, use my shoulder," Steven offered.

He stared at the house for a long while. He'd do something about her bitching too, and he'd do it soon. Finally he accepted the boy's offer of help and with his right arm over Steven's shoulder for a crutch, he hobbled toward the house. He had to do something soon about that woman's mouth.

"We'll have to kill him, won't we?" Steven asked as he carefully sought places for him to step.

"Maybe, maybe not. I'll think on it awhile. We best not speak of it around her."

"Oh, I won't."

"Well, you could have learned more from a post than

he told you,'' she announced as they gathered for supper after a worthless session interrogating the federal man.

"Did you lock him in good?" Rafter asked his eldest while scowling after Barbara.

"He ain't going nowhere," Arland said.

"He does," she began, "they'll have the whole damn army up here. They killed a federal tax man once in Tennessee when I was a girl and the feds came in and they hung twelve bootleggers to get the right one."

"They won't never find his body. Shut up about him!" Rafter said, the whiskey not cutting the pain.

"Mark my words—"

"I said to shut up!" He raised his arm to threaten her.

"You ain't my master!"

"You keep on, woman. I'll show you who's the master." He wagged his index finger at her.

She stalked off. He lifted his pain-filled right leg, hoping for a more comfortable position.

"You boys can serve the food," he said. That leg was going to kill him. He rocked back and forth on his butt in the kitchen chair as he squeezed it between both hands. He never should have ridden with them down there, but they needed leadership. They'd only shot around without him to tell them what to do, like burning that damn wagon and taking that federal man prisoner. The trip had only worsened his condition.

"Get me some whiskey!" He had to have some relief.

"Pa, there's only this bottle left," Steven said, coming from the cupboard.

"You boys been in my whiskey?" There should have been two more bottles. Those boys knew better than to tap his supply. She'd drunk it!

"We don't ever touch it," Ned said, waited for his father's nod, and then took his plate and went outside.

Rafter cut the seal on the bottle with his jackknife. When those boys left in the morning, he'd settle with her on several scores. He popped out the cork and then put the glass rim to his mouth and upended it. He needed lots of whiskey.

In the light of dawn Slocum walked down the roan horse. After many close encounters where the gelding sniffed at his hand, then bolted away, Slocum finally captured the short coupled horse and led him back to his saddle and bedroll. Saddled, he swung up and went to survey the damage. Dead sheep lay across the sagebrush-studded land. Hundred, by his count. The survivors, crying lambs searching for their mothers who died, or ewes plaintively bleating and looking for a lost baby.

Both dogs lay dead not fifty feet from the burned-out camp wagon. He would never be required to drive it again. Both donkeys rose from grazing and brayed at him as if they wanted to say something. He turned and wondered about Tad Markum.

First he must find her. Then he would track down where they'd taken Tad. Guilt-laden, he had not slept since the raid, and wondered over and over how he might have avoided the young man's capture and the senseless sheep slaughter. No answer surfaced; he rose in the stirrups and trotted the roan.

At midmorning he spotted her and some riders. He made the gelding lope and drew him up short of her and the three Navaho boys on colorful paints.

"What's wrong?" she asked. The pained look on her face hurt him.

"They attacked the camp last night without warning. Burned the wagon, shot the dogs. Took Tad prisoner."

She shook her head, speechless. "Why—"

"Taking Tad prisoner might be my fault. For effect, after they denied you credit, you recall I told that bunch at the store, Tad was a federal tax man. I never dreamed it would put him in such jeopardy."

"The flock?"

"They shot several head. There were too many for me

to stop them, I'm sorry." He couldn't look at her, he'd let both her and Tad down.

"Slocum, don't blame yourself. What are you going to do next?" she asked.

"I've wondered all night. First, I'm going to try to find Tad."

"I'm going with you."

"Why don't you go to your father and clear out." He looked at her, so pained by the turn of events beyond his control, he hoped to change her answer.

"No," she said, and turned to the eldest of the three Navahos. "Charlie, you and the boys gather the sheep that are left and take them to Lee's Ferry. The captain will give you food on my credit. I will be along later."

"We can do that," the boy said, and then he translated to the other two, who looked to be in their mid-teens.

"They will be hard to drive," Slocum said, "without the dogs."

Charlie dismissed his concern with a shake of his head.

"Charlie is a good herder," she said, turning back to Slocum. "He'll do a good job. I'm ready to ride."

"I can't change your mind?"

"No, you can't."

"What about your father?"

"Mrs. Gray will look after him."

Slocum studied the towering bloodred face of the Vermilion Cliffs. He couldn't sway her for anything. Fine, they would ride to Joseph's Lake and somehow learn where Tad was being held. After they secured his release, he planned to dish out some of his own venom in return for last night's devastation. He wasn't certain how—he just knew he would find a way.

10

"Paw, Steven can stay and help you guard that prisoner," Arland offered. Ned and Steven both nodded as they waited for his reply. The three were mounted and leading a pack-horse loaded with supplies and ready to ride out.

"No, we need that stock run down in the low country. We're late, kinda slid by me, the time, I mean. You boys will need them extra horses of ours up on Wolf Tongue. Just be careful and don't take no flights like I did."

They laughed and headed out. He looked at the smoke house; the door was barred. He would see about that federal man later. Taking him prisoner hadn't set well with the others, but they had no guts. He needed more whiskey and she'd drunk it. Damn her contrary soul, he was fed up with her mouthing too.

He studied the high, wispy clouds. Weather would soon change, this warm weather wouldn't last. Damn shame cows were too stupid to migrate. They'd been lucky no longer than the snow had lasted last time. It would soon set in and stay. The boys had time to get most of the cattle off the mountain if they hurried.

He limped in the front door, wondering where she was at. He finally sat down in the stuffed chair and swung his bad leg up on the ladderback.

"Woman, bring me some more coffee!" he shouted.

No answer. He considered getting up, but there was no need, she could bring him some. She must be out tending her chickens. When she got back, he'd have her bring the pot in there.

The sound of her rattling pans in the kitchen awoke him from a nap. "Bring the coffeepot in here."

He heard it clang, and, satisfied, held out his cup for her to refill it.

"You figure on sitting around all the time?" she demanded.

"What do you mean?" Hell, he had a broken leg, what did she expect?

"It can't hurt worse than having a baby. I got up from that the next day and cooked and sewed."

"This here leg is broke and swollen."

"You say." She whirled and went into the kitchen.

"By damn, it is broken and swollen—" She was out of sight, and besides, she didn't care about his suffering. He shifted some in the chair and flinched at the deep pain in his leg.

He dozed and awoke. What was left of the whiskey barely helped his suffering. Until he went to Joseph's Lake, he would have no more painkiller. Maybe he'd chew boot leather; they gave that to men they operated on during the war.

He hobbled across the room and out on the porch to relieve himself. Intent on directing his stream off the edge, he glanced at the smoke house. The bar across the door was down. He blinked again, realizing what was wrong across the yard. He hastily buttoned up his pants. That dude could never have gotten the bar off. Someone had released him.

"Barbara!" he screamed, dragging his leaden leg as he crossed the yard and threw open the smoke-house door. Just as he suspected, the federal man was gone. She'd turned him out! Why? By gawd, he'd had enough. Where was he? Greenhorn fool couldn't go far; he'd better go back to the house and get his gun.

He hopped along, out of breath, then the bad leg crumpled under him. Filled with fury, he bellied down and crawled on his hands and one leg back inside the house and pulled himself up on a chair to finally stand before the gun rack. He took the .44/40 from the rack and levered a shell into the chamber.

A step, a pain to swing the dead weight around, then another step, and another swing. He had to find that federal man and kill him. He couldn't allow him to make a report on the Kiabab. The hurt shot into his hip socket as he swung the sore leg around again and again.

He covered the ground to the horse shed as quickly as his limb would let him. Then he ducked down, looking for the man. He wouldn't go far, he'd soon be lost in the timber or fall off into the Grand Canyon. Good enough for him too.

Grunting and straining, he moved around the shed, hoping to find the federal man either shivering behind a bush or ready to give up when the gun barrel was pointed at him. He'd need to make him dig his own grave. No way he could do a damn thing.

He leaned his shoulder to the rough logs for support and let his racing heart catch up. His ragged breath whistled through his throat. She must have let that bar down. No way anyone else would have done it.

Rafter listened. Was there someone running? He heard rapid footsteps. In his haste he forgot about his bad leg and the pain, the momentum carrying him around past the corrals. When his bad leg finally gave out under him, he toppled and began rolling downhill over and over until he lodged against a large clump of sage. He was grateful that despite the hard spill he still held the rifle as he lay on his side. He tried to clear his head; the fall had swirled his brain.

He tried to shake away the dizziness and see the escapee. The horses in the lot snorted and blew dust. Someone was up there, trying to mount.

He fought with the action of the rifle, ejecting a shell, in his haste forgetting the rifle was loaded and slamming another round in. Then he heard the drum of hooves and his good sorrel horse Buddy sailed over the corral fence with a hatless man aboard.

"Damn," he swore out loud as he rolled over, trying to get the rider in his sights as the sorrel bounded over sagebrush, going down the mountain into the timber. He should have shot the horse. The escapee had gotten away on one of his best horses. He closed his eyes to the raging fire in his leg.

Damn her—she let him out. He lay back, the rifle slipping from his grasp as tears ran down his face. Nothing ever hurt this badly.

"Barbara! Barbara!" He beat the ground with his fists. Why didn't she come out and help him? He squalled out her name until he was hoarse. He crawled a few feet farther and then blacked out from the pain.

How long he had laid on the hard ground, he was unsure, But he began his return to the house inch by inch, crawling. Out of breath, he paused many times. The rifle was too short to become a crutch. He pulled it along as he made the snaillike trip.

Uphill was slow going, and he fainted into unconsciousness for over an hour on the ground beside the barn. Twilight had come and gone before he finally made the porch. Inside the dark house he used a kitchen chair for a crutch. He went down the hall, clanking along.

She must be in bed. All day she had known he was out there, helpless. She hadn't even called him for supper. He pushed open the door to her room and the chair thudded on the floor. No light was necessary. The starlight coming in the window was enough. The chair pounded on the flooring when he swung it ahead and twisted his body to bring the bloated leg after him step by step.

"This is my room. Get out!" she said.

His breath whistled through his nose. Under his shirt, his surging heart raged in his chest from the strenuous effort. He saw her sitting up in the bed. Good, she was over there.

"You hear me!" she threatened.

He never answered her. His knees were finally against her bed at last. All day he fought to get back to the house—all day he dreamed of standing by the bed, a riding quirt in his hand, ready to beat her until she cried.

"I won't stand for this—"

The hell you won't! He jerked the feather pillow up and then dove at her. She screamed, kicked, fought, and finally squirmed as he forced the pillow over her face, but her efforts were all for naught. He had her mouth covered and his weight was more than she could escape. Harder and harder he pressed down on the pillow.

"You knew I was out there!" he raged. "You turned him loose! You let him go! All day I have crawled like a dog to get back here! You never helped me! You deserve to die!"

Her muffled protest grew weaker. Her skinny arms that tried to pry his grip loose grew weaker, and he used more force to press the pillow down even harder. At last her body went limp. He did not quit holding it down for a long while.

Finally satisfied she was dead, he rose, the rivers of sweat running down his face. He tossed the pillow to the head of the bed. Shaken, he backed up until his good leg was on the floor. He would bury her later. Somehow he had made it back to the house. He could do that too. But he had to rest for a while first. Killing her had been harder than he thought it would be. The room began to swirl. He dropped heavily to the bed and then passed out.

•　•　•

Slocum motioned for Matty to stay back. They were closing in on the drunken man who swayed as he walked away from the general store down the dim road in the starlight.

"Going home—I'm—going home."

Slocum had him from behind with an arm around his neck and his skinning knife pressed to his throat.

"Don't move an inch," he said in the man's ear. He could smell the sourness of his breath.

"I ain't. What do you want?"

"Where is the federal man you kidnapped?"

"I never done it. No part of it, killing them sheep was bad enough. Mercy, that was mean and awful. Why, them Sikeses gone crazy."

"Who?"

"Rafter Sikes."

"Where's he at?"

"At his ranch, I reckon. I never harmed a hair on that boy's head. I said twice for them to let him go."

"Can you run?"

"Pretty good, why?"

" 'Cause if you aren't out of sight in two shakes, I am going to cut off both your ears."

"Sweet Jesus, please, mister, don't do that. I admit I shot them sheep, but I never liked it none—"

"Run!"

"Oh!" He ran down the road into the darkness, wailing at the top of his lungs.

"Did you learn where he's at?" she asked.

"Sikes's ranch is where they're holding him, near as he knew."

"That's south, below Mount Trumbull."

"You ever been there?" he asked, watching to see if anyone came out of the store to check on the hollering drunk.

"No, but we can find it."

"I suspect the way he talked that Sikes was the one who wanted Tad held prisoner." He reached out and caught her arm. "Wait, you are only a few miles from your headquarters. Why don't you stay with your father."

She threw her arms around his neck. "I am going with you."

Then she stood on her toes and kissed him. A kiss of importance, not a fleeting one, not a grateful one, but one that sent messages to his brain. The urgency of her mouth caused him to wrap his arms around her tighter and hold her form to his body.

They finally broke for air.

"We better ride," he said in her ear. The muscles in his arms trembled as he released her. For a moment they looked into each other's eyes. There would be time later— he would find the time later.

They rode at a trot. The south road cut through the ponderosa forest, swirled in inky darkness, opened to meadows bathed in pearly starlight. He fretted about Tad's safety as they rode, so they weren't too late to save the Yale man. They startled browsing mule deer that snorted and then broke off into the boughs of the surrounding pines to escape.

Hours and many miles later, their horses grew weary and snorted in the dust. He halted her and they rode off the road into a clearing. There he unsaddled his horse and helped her with hers. The tired animals would not venture far. He unfurled his ground cloth and then the blankets.

She tackled him by the waist and buried her face in his vest. They slunk to the bedroll, kissed, and fell fast asleep in each other's arms.

11

Rafter Sikes awoke with a start and barely opened his right eye. Daylight streamed into the room. She lay not six inches from his face, her purple lips set in a tight, compressed line, her dull eyes staring at the ceiling. The deep blue spider veins shined through the translucent skin on her temple. He drew back slowly, afraid she might awaken from the dead. Uglier in death than she was alive, but her mouth was silent.

How long had he been asleep? Slept with her, no less. He hadn't been in bed with her in over a decade. She'd been dead that last time too. He began to realize how much his right leg hurt, how the aching never left him. He used both hands to lift and swing it off the bed. Then, with the chair as his support, he clunked off to relieve himself and to find something to eat.

He didn't bother to look back at her from the bedroom doorway. He'd tell the boys she must have had a heart attack—a stroke. He'd tell them that he found her in bed, dead, that morning.

He needed to silence that federal man too. If he didn't,

he would bring the U.S. Marshals in. The tenderfoot that got away didn't know beans about the country he was headed into. He'd get lost in those canyons. They twisted and turned until you could see your own ass at times.

Secondly, the Grand Canyon itself was impossible to cross. Still, to be certain the man never returned, he'd need to saddle a horse and go after him. In the meantime there was the dead Barbara to think about. He'd cover her up with a sheet, have the boys come back so they could dig the damn grave. The federal man was the only hitch in his plans; those McArthurs had to get out or he'd kill them too. After he got rid of them and his leg healed, he'd go up to Cedar City and bring Naoma home.

He ate some dry corn bread he found in the kitchen. No time to stoke up a stove and make coffee, he had to catch up with the federal man and get rid of him. The dry bread caked in his mouth as he took the rifle, using the chair for a crutch, and went outside.

Somehow he needed to capture a gentle horse, get in the saddle, and track down the pilgrim. He couldn't chance him not dying, though he would surely be killed by exposure, hunger, or thirst. With the ladderback chair for support, he made it to the barn. Then, out of breath, he rested. He would need to rope a horse from outside the corral.

Maybe a pail of feed would coax one over. He worked with his chair over to the bins, filled a bucket, and hobbled back.

"Here," he said, unlatching the gate and barring any escape.

Possum, a good choice for him to ride, came over and sniffed suspiciously, but another horse ran in and nipped him on the ribs. Possum bolted away.

"Stop your damn fighting!" he shouted. His loud words spooked the horses back and he looked to the sky for assistance. "Come here, you stupid bangtails, I've got miles to ride."

He finally coaxed Shorty up to the feed and managed to

get a rope around his throat. With great effort he finally got his chair turned in the opposite direction. Shorty acted stupid at the sight of this contraption and nearly pulled loose. But he managed to lead him out and close the gate, then coaxed him over to the saddle and bridle.

However, when he went to mount him, Shorty would not stand close enough to the chair for him to get on. He kept circling and looking with suspicion at the arrangement.

"Dammit! Shorty, it's only a kitchen chair. Whoa, you dumb idiot."

Finally, using his good knee, he managed to stand on the seat and led the horse up, but each time Shorty sidled away when he tried to ease over on his back. He feared reaching for the horn—the bay might spook and jerk him off and dump him on the ground.

After numerous tries he was able to slip in the saddle. The shock of the drop into the seat sent stars bursting inside his skull. In his pain he reined the horse so hard and sudden, the pony responded by jerking backward and knocking open the gate with his rump.

"Whoa!" he shouted. No time to close it. He would have to dismount to manage the heavy pole gate. Damn, his spare saddle horses would be scattered to Christmas. What else?

He nudged Shorty over so he could pick up the rifle by the muzzle. But he couldn't use his right heel. That leg for his purposes was dead. So he repeatedly reined and tried to make the bay horse get closer to where the Winchester leaned against the feed box.

"Get over here, stupid!" He reached so far, he pulled the muscles in the sore right leg and still could not grasp the gun; then the pain forced him to stop.

"I need that gun, you dumb bastard." In desperation, he rode outside and came back inside, making the bay heel over with his left foot. With a sigh of relief, at last he reached down, hoisted the rifle up by the barrel, shoved it in the boot, and then turned the gelding out.

He dropped down the hill to find the man's tracks. When he looked back in disgust, he saw a half dozen saddle horses running six different directions.

Dawn through the ponderosa boughs shattered Slocum's sleep. The nearby horses chomped on grass. He rose on an elbow to look around. Nothing seemed out of place as shafts of golden sunlight gilded the small meadow. He gazed down at his bed partner, listened to the gentle whisper of her breath as she slept.

"It's morning," he whispered.

From somewhere on high, a saucy jay scolded them for oversleeping. Three raucous magpies echoed the jay's sentiments.

"Wow, it's morning," she said, and stretched her arms out over her head.

"You sleep good?"

"Yes. Did you?"

"Oh, yes. We need to get going," he said.

She wrinkled her nose mischievously at him and then shook her head. "Come here."

He bent over to kiss her. Then his left arm snaked under her neck, and they were soon packed together, tasting each other, hungry for more.

He rolled her easily on top of him and they locked mouths, seeking each other's source. He undid her divided skirt and she rose to shed it. With a mischievous grin she unbuttoned his shirt and then sat on him and laughed aloud as she removed her blouse.

"Wicked, aren't I?"

"Beautiful, not wicked," he whispered, reaching up for her.

He pulled her down and explored her hard breasts through the thin cotton camisole. She pursed her lips for him, and he sought them. The newfound fire spread the flames of desire through them. His pants were soon gone.

She stripped his one-piece underwear off his shoulders with her small, callused hands.

He slipped over her.

"I'm afraid," she said softly. He could feel her tremble; concern clouded her brown eyes.

"Don't be, this isn't revenge."

"I know, Slocum," she said, and tears began to spill from her eyes. "Please don't stop, I can't help this."

He spread her legs apart and moved inside them. He sought her with care. Her hands tightly clutched his hips, then, as entry passed, she sighed in relief, released him, and threw her head back to savor the depth of his intrusion.

"Yes, yes," she whispered.

An inferno rose to meet him. He savored her subtle body, her hard legs wrapped around him. She raised her slim hips up for more as they both rode the tempest waves on the sea of passion.

There was no Kiabab Plateau, no turpentine smell of woods in the air, no soft, cool breeze on their skin. They were a million miles away on top of fluffy clouds, drunk on the wines of erotic notions, fulfilled only by the charging force of their willing bodies to become one.

Finally spent, too weak to move, they lay in each other's arms, goose bumps on their skin as the chill of the morning swept over their nakedness.

He reached for the displaced cover and swung it over them.

She mumbled, "Thanks, I knew it had to be different," and then nestled closer to his chest.

Later they shared some tepid, metallic-tasting water from Slocum's canteen. He tossed on their saddles, Matty packed up the bedroll, and they rode south on the dim road.

An hour later she pointed to a sign nailed onto a tree trunk. It was a board with a WTS brand and an arrow.

"Lucky we didn't ride by it last night," he said, and stood in the stirrups to look off the mountain where the two tracks twisted out of his view. He hated to ride into a trap. If Sikes had any lookouts posted, or dogs, they would warn the man. Still, daylight was burning and they needed to find Tad. If the Sikeses ever tired of him, one of them might have the nerve to shoot him in cold blood. He hoped not.

The canyon they rode down was narrow. She pointed out tall Mount Trumbull to the east. The road was hardly more than two tracks. It was seldom used by a wagon. Several horses had recently gone out this way. The fresher horse apples looked a day old to him.

"I hope they weren't taking Tad somewhere else."

They rode up without incident or challenge to the barn, eyeing the house for any sign and seeing nothing. They dismounted and Slocum motioned for Matty to stay back. The Colt in his hand, Slocum stood by the side of the barn. He could see through the cracks; there was no one inside the pole structure,

Who was at the main house? The front door was wide open. Still, he was skeptical. There was no time to waste, so he decided to break for the porch. He frowned at the strange tracks in the dust as he crossed the yard. Four sticks, it looked like, set equally apart.

On the porch he held his breath, listened for any sound, and then waved for Matty to stay back. The Colt in his hand and ready, he moved swiftly inside. He paused to check for sounds—nothing.

No one in the kitchen, the stove was cold. He worked his way down the hallway. From the doorway he saw the still woman on the bed and realized she was dead. He stepped in close and saw no wounds. Died of something else, he decided, pulling the sheet over her.

"Slocum, come out here," Matty shouted.

He rushed outside and saw her on her knees at the small outbuilding.

"These are Tad's bootprints in the dust. I'd know them anywhere. They must have kept him in this building. What's in the house?"

"A dead woman." Slocum surveyed the yard and tried to imagine what had happened.

"Oh," she said with a frown. "Who is it?"

He shrugged. "Could be his wife. She died of something, no wounds."

"She been dead long?"

"No, maybe a day or since last night. I wonder where they took Tad?" He looked around at the signs in the dust, then, convinced that the barn held some answers, headed there.

"Where are you going?"

"To try and figure out these holes," he said, and began to track the marks.

When he discovered the ladderback chair in the barn, he knew what had made the marks.

"Someone used that chair for a crutch from the house to here. See where they dragged a boot along." He pointed. "They must have used it to get on a horse. See all the prints here by the same animal."

"Who needed it?"

"I wish that dead woman could talk." Slocum scouted outside the barn.

"Where did he ride that horse?" she asked.

"Strange, he went down this bank and south," he said, scooting on his bootheels off the bank to follow the fresh tracks.

"What are we going to do?" she asked from above.

"Get the horses. I have notion these prints may lead us to something."

"I'll be right there," she said, and ran off for their mounts.

Farther along the slope, he found where someone had dragged himself up the hillside. Whoever was crippled had spent a lot of time on his belly, pulling himself up the grade. It was not the woman; these tracks were made by a large man.

"Find anything else?" she asked, riding her pony and leading his roan.

"Someone crawled on his belly out of here."

"Why was that?"

"I'm not certain, but I figure whoever was crippled and got on that chair must be the same one."

She rode down the hillside. "Two sets of horse hooves down here."

Slocum stayed on the slope. "Come this way. Does one set come down this hill?"

"Yes, it does."

He shielded his eyes against the sun and looked up toward the corrals. "I'd say someone took a horse out of those pens and he jumped over the fence and charged off down through here."

"The Yale man?"

"He's probably rode hunters before."

"What's wrong?" she asked as he hurried down the slope.

"If we're wrong and they took him out on the road, it may cost him his life."

"Chance we have to take," she said.

He agreed, then he swung in the saddle in a bound and set the roan off the mountain. They slipped downhill through the tall pines. The trail was dim, but signs of prints still showed. It was on a point that Matty discovered the bootprint. She leaned over to study it and finally dismounted to verify her find.

"It's his round-toed boot all right," she said, excited, and her voice echoed across the deep chasm that they rode along the side of the mountain.

"Someone is tracking him. I think it's the cripple."

"That's not so bad."

"Maybe not, but Tad's not a western man. If he can survive and dodge whoever is on his back trail, he may stand a chance." Slocum booted his horse downhill.

"Slocum, can we go faster?"

"Not much," he said, worried about the two of them riding into a trap.

The morning fled and they pushed deeper into the broken canyon country. Afternoon lengthened, and Slocum found fresh signs. He scoured the steep slopes above them and the tall timber for any hint of a sniper or a trap. They chewed on his peppery jerky as they rode. Matty even twisted and turned in the saddle, watching for an ambush.

"This country gets tougher," she said from behind him as they rode single file on the rocky trail. It pitched sharply downhill, and he hoped there would be water at the bottom.

"It isn't for the faint at heart," he said over his shoulder.

"Poor Yale man, he's sure getting himself a real taste of the West."

"Just so he survives it," Slocum said, and leaned back as the roan descended an extra steep stretch.

12

"He's somewhere in this canyon," Rafter said aloud to himself as he scrubbed his mouth on his palm. He reached back and drew out the .44/40 and rested the butt on the saddle swell.

The tracks were plain enough. The tenderfoot had ridden Buddy off the mountain and down into the canyon. Hadn't figured he would ever get this far. Rafter had expected to find him lying along the trail, starving and out of water. He hated to underestimate any enemy, but this was a tenderfoot and he aimed to bag him before dark.

He didn't dare get off his horse either. Kind of gave the dude a bigger chance. Of course, the pilgrim had no weapon. No food in a day and half. They hadn't fed him at the ranch. Maybe two days without food. However, he probably found some canned goods in the smoke house.

The damn corn cakes she left for him had been piss-poor, dry eating. Lucky for him, he had some crackers and hard cheese in his saddlebags that he'd bought last time he swung by the Joseph's Lake store on the way to the sheep raid. He booted the bay on, searching the brush along the shallow creek. Pools of silver water dotted the sandy wash. They tempted him as he rode down the bottom.

He rode on. He'd been in worse shape before. Hunting this dude had made him forget about his leg, though any jarring sent plenty of pain up his side. His pain wasn't going to detour him from finding this damn tenderfoot and nailing his hide up. He thought of Naoma. She was young enough, they might even have some kids. With Barbara out of the way, and this sheep thing nearly settled, he could concentrate on other things.

Finish off this federal man and he'd head for Wolf Tongue and let the boys wait on him and his bum leg. Soon as that was mended, he'd ride up to Cedar City and check on Naoma. Be a lot better if she'd been home when he fell off the mountain. Still, it didn't matter, it would all work out. He'd get his good horse Buddy back and soon be headed for the line shack.

He send the bay busting through the stream and up the far bank. Then he spotted the sorrel, and a rider from the corner of his eyes burst out of the willows. He drew the rifle up and strained to find the red horse in his sights and then he looked for the rider low on his back.

The gun roared, but he knew when he pulled the trigger that he'd missed. He didn't want to hit the good horse and he'd shot too high. Cursing his bad luck, he reined the excited bay around and sent him down the sandy bank. He had the dude bottled up in this canyon, and it was only a matter of time until he closed the jaws of his trap.

He loped the bay along the side of the stream in the sand. Where had that sum bitch gone anyway? No matter, he had seen him and now all he needed to do was find and kill him.

"You hear a shot?" Slocum asked, turning his ear to listen for another.

Woodenly, Matty nodded when he turned to look at her.

"You better stay up here," he said, trying to see into the canyon below them.

"Slocum, you couldn't make me stay here if you had a rope to tie me up with."

"I'll handle this."

"Good, I'll be there if you need any help."

"You're hardheaded."

"Takes one to know one."

He didn't bother to answer that. He wanted to go faster but knew the roan was doing all he could. Soon they'd be in the bottoms and the steep trail would be over. He listened intently for more shots. He hoped they weren't too late.

At the stream Slocum spotted the fresh tracks. The long shadows of evening were engulfing the canyon. Another hour of light, maybe less, as the sun shone on the peaks above them. He drew his Colt and send the roan off in a dead run down the stream bed.

Another shot rang out and he reined up.

"You stay back," he said. For whatever good that did, he spurred the roan on down the bottoms. He could see well enough if there was a horse and rider.

Maybe they hadn't killed the young man yet. Two shots didn't mean much—one shot could have done him in. The roan horse was stretched out. Water flew in a high spray when he busted through the shallow puddles.

A gunshot broke the air and Slocum felt the gelding falter. He shook his boots free of the stirrups, realizing that the horse had been struck. The cow pony went down to his knees, still running, the impact spilling Slocum over his head and facedown onto the sand. This bastard had shot his horse. He scrambled in the loose sand for the cover of the low bank, anger tightening his jaw muscles.

He heard her scream. Disregarding his own safety, he rose to look for her.

"Get back!" he shouted.

The next bullet sounded, and he saw her short coupled pony fall over on his right side to the ground. Slocum cursed as he rose to look for the shooter. Shooting at him was one thing, but to deliberately gun down a mount from under a woman was more than he could tolerate.

He raced for Matty, concerned she was pinned under the horse, blasting away with his Colt despite the distance to the man on the bay. Slocum was grateful when the shooter turned tail in the face of someone returning his fire and rode hell-bent for the mountain. Full out, he sped on his boot soles to check on her condition.

"Get down." She waved from beyond the fallen horse.

He drew up, satisfied she wasn't hurt, and watched the shooter's horse cat-hop up the trail they'd just come down.

"It was him," she said, still on her side with her right leg pinned under the dead pony.

"Who?" he asked, examining the situation.

"Rafter Sikes."

Slocum cast a hard look in that direction. The shooter was gone, but he would pay and pay dearly for doing this to her. He settled his butt on the ground close beside her, braced himself, and put both feet against the saddle horn. With all his might he shoved until she managed to draw her foot out from underneath the dead cow pony.

"You all right?" he asked, out of breath and on all fours beside her.

Tears began to well out of her eyes as she hugged his neck.

"I'm fine, but poor Tad," she sobbed. "We're too late for him."

He patted her on the back. Nothing much that they could do afoot, they were in a real pickle. Yes, sir, that Sikes would pay dearly for this.

"Anyone got something to eat?" a cheery voice asked.

"What?" they both said, falling from their hug.

"Thank God you two came along. Sorry about him shooting your horses, but I damn sure am glad to see the likes of you two."

"Tad? Oh, how did you ever make it?" she asked, scrambling to her feet.

"Just my dumb luck," he said as she hugged him, and she cried some more. "Wouldn't you call it that, Slocum?" he asked.

"I would, friend. I would indeed call it luck." He studied the dark timber on the slope as twilight settled in. One good thing, their Yale man was safe.

13

They scraped up enough dry wood for a fire. Although convinced by Tad's evaluation of the condition of Rafter Sikes's leg, that he was not liable to return, still, as the stars came out, Slocum kept an eye on the mountain and an ear for any sign of a returning rider.

He located a few coffee beans in his saddlebag. Matty handed out jerky while they boiled the water in two tin cans and used Slocum's cup to share the precious drink. He saved a portion of the ground beans for the morning.

A wolf began to howl and she moved closer to him without a word, but he saw the uneasiness on her face lighted by the campfire.

"I doubt he comes nearer than that," he said. "Besides, there's enough deer to occupy him."

"I wish I was as certain as you are," she said, handing the cup over to Tad.

"He ain't hungry enough to even venture within a hundred yards of this fire," Slocum said.

"Good, stay up there, wolf. You ever get all the cat hair out of your mouth?" she teased him.

"I think so."

"That wolf didn't eat me last night," Tad said.

"That was a long night too, wasn't it?" she asked.

"That ain't the half of it."

"You did good not to lose your head through all of this, Tad. You said his wife was the one that let you out of the smoke house?" Slocum tried to fathom why.

Tad shrugged and passed the cup back to Slocum.

"She told me to run. Said that he'd sure kill me and he'd probably kill her too for letting me out. Something about not having a federal man's death on her hands."

"She's dead," Matty said. "Slocum found her in the house."

"Oh, that's too bad. Did he kill her?"

"I didn't see any wounds. She was just dead in her night-gown in the bed."

"What next?" Matty asked.

"Get some sleep and we'll walk back to the WTS and confiscate some fresh horses, then ride to Joseph's Lake."

"Do what there?" Matty asked.

"Someone needs to go alert the authorities."

She shook her head ruefully. "What'll they do, come over here and tell the Sikeses to stop shooting at us and the flock?"

"That along with kidnapping and attempted murder are serious charges."

"He'll just buy his way out of it."

"Then there's one way to stop them."

"How's that?" Tad asked.

"Bury them." Slocum drew a cigar out of his vest, flicked a match head alive with his thumbnail, struck the blaze to the cigar, and drew in deeply. The warm smoke settled some of the fire inside him, but not all of it.

It wasn't far to Wolf Tongue, Rafter kept reminding himself over and over again as he rode through the inky night, fighting his need for sleep and jerking himself upright as his head drooped. No matter that he had to find the boys, he'd bought some time shooting their horses out from under them. That gunman and the girl—McArthur's daughter, Matty. Those boys didn't do her much good, raping her. He'd thought she'd left the country by this time. They needed to get all three of them—his boys needed to get all three for him, that federal man, her, and the gunman.

It was getting colder by the hour, and a storm was coming. His leg pained him as if someone were beating on it every minute with a sledgehammer. No time for self-indulgence, he had to make the line shack and get those boys on the trail of those three. They could always steal new cattle up in Utah or someplace. Those three—had they come back by the house? Found Barb's corpse? They couldn't tell anything. She had a stroke, yes, he was certain she'd had a bad one.

Poor woman, and in his condition he'd never had a chance to bury her. Be lots better, though, if she was in the ground. There'd be less questions to answer. He'd had no time to swing back. Besides, if he ever got off this horse, without help he'd never get back on. It couldn't be many more miles. Damn, he was groggy.

With a death grip on the saddle horn, he tried to shake his head and clear out the drowsiness. No good, he had to—

"Paw, that you?" Steven shouted.

"Yeah, old Shorty got me here," he said, almost not believing it.

"Yeah, old Shorty brung you. Paw, what are you doing riding out here this time of the night anyway?"

"Where's Arland and Ned?" he asked.

"Aw, they rode over to see if some widow woman was back."

"You didn't go?" he asked, laying his arm over the boy's shoulder. Slowly, he took little steps toward the shack.

"Naw, besides, it's a long ride over and back, and she might not even be back from Cedar City."

"Oh," he said, and winced at the pain from his foot. Damn, she'd never mentioned his boys coming by her place. He'd have to straighten that out when he took her to the ranch.

"They go to see her often?" he asked.

"Often enough when she's at home."

"Oh, yeah, well, I've got some bad news." He paused at the front steps. Despite the cold night air, he was sweating. Dragging his bad leg was tough enough, he had to watch real carefully what he said—about Naoma and Barbara's death as well.

"What's that?"

"Your maw's dead. She must of had a stroke while she slept. Found her dead in bed in the morning."

"Oh, that's bad. She was fine the day we left."

"I know, must have been her heart. We'll all miss her, but she never suffered. Might be for the best."

"I guess. You hungry? I got some stew left."

"I could eat a bear, son. Ain't had nothing to eat in two days."

"My gosh, she never fed you."

"No, I think she knew she was kinda sick."

"Paw, what did you do with that federal man?"

He eased himself down on the rough bench and adjusted his bad leg. There was no place comfortable for it. Cold chills ran up his face until finally the pain in his hip subsided enough so he could breathe again.

"That's why I come after you boys, he got away."

"Got away?"

"Yes. And we've got to get him before he tells the law on us."

"Ned and Arland get back, we'll go find him."

"I knew you would." He spooned up some of the stew the boy had brought him from the pot on the stove. Steven was a good boy, he'd taken his mother's death better than he expected. She was gone, and that was it. He should have killed her years before. The sharpness of a knife in his leg caused him to clench up—that blasted thing would be the death of him yet.

"You all right, Paw?"

"I will be," he said, strained. "I will be."

They'd hiked since before dawn. She rode the big sorrel while Tad and Slocum walked along behind.

"Law out here is sure different than home in Pennsylvania."

"Ha, we don't even have law out here," she said over her shoulder.

"There's always law," Slocum said. "It's made by whoever is in charge."

"Rafter Sikes's law?" she asked, twisting in the saddle to look at them. She bore Slocum's rig in her lap. He hated to leave behind a perfectly good saddle in the canyon.

"Yes, even his law. But we're going to change some thinking when we get back," Slocum said.

"How is that?" she asked.

"You believe in ghosts?"

"Never seen one I thought was real."

"These will be," Slocum said. "Matty, you start making me a list of these guys that you think joined Sikes in the sheep raid."

"Lord, that could be as long as your arm."

"Start working on it," Slocum said.

"What are you going to do?" Tad asked.

Slocum searched the timbered slopes for any sign of Sikes. Then he looked back into the deep canyon, grateful they were so far out of the bottom.

"Well, like this, we're going to rig us up some real spooky things. They'll get the message quick enough."

"I'm game to help you."

"Good, we need some white paint, some sheets, some rope, and some pulleys."

"I don't know how you're going to spook grown men," she said.

"You wait and see."

"How do we start?" she said. "We've got all that at the ranch."

"Good, you think of the names."

"Kelly Blue, for one."

"Yes, I heard them holler his name out the night they attacked the flock." Tad said. "They called him Blue this and that."

"Good, he'll be the first one we spook."

"How we going to do it?"

"You'll see," Slocum promised, not entirely certain of his whole plan.

"Why don't we simply get Sikes?" she asked.

"We need to cut off Sikes from the others."

"And scaring them will do that?"

"Yes, ma'am," he said, wiping his sweaty forehead on his sleeve. Hot for this time of year, a change would soon be coming, late as it was.

14

"Kelly? Kelly Blue?" The voice waved off into the night.

"Kelly, wake up," a woman's voice said sharply inside the house. "Some damned old drunk cowboy is outside in the yard, hollering for you."

"I never heard him."

"I did! Go see who it is."

"Hellfire, woman, them dogs would be raising hell if anyone was out there."

"Them dogs is all asleep."

"Not my damn dogs, I got the best damn watchdogs—"

Behind him one of the six bound and muzzled dogs in the wagon whimpered. Slocum waited. Soon the tall, lean figure in his underwear came charging out on the house, tripped over the thin string, and sprawled facedown into the dirt in front of the porch.

"Kelly?" the voice wavered.

"Damn, who's out there?" He was on all fours.

"The ghost of the dead sheep!"

"I don't believe in ghosts!"

"We are the ghosts and we've come to eat your lawn."

99

"Here, Rip! Here, Joe!" he called to his dogs, still on all fours on the ground. "Ain't no damn sheep eating my lawn, no, sir. Who the hell are you? What did you do to my damn dogs?"

"They have gone to their death, like you will if you don't stop killing sheep."

"Listen, I ain't afraid of you. No, sir."

"Kelly, who's out there?" his wife hissed from the porch.

"I swear, Ruby, I don't know, but they've got my damn dogs and they say they're ghost sheep going to graze my yard."

"Well, why don't you get up?" she asked.

"I ain't sure."

"Come inside," she commanded.

He began to scurry for the door. He was on the porch when he began to scream. "Dammit, Ruby, they done been here already! Already, they've been here!"

"How do you know?" she cried out, dragging him in the doorway and slamming it shut.

"I've got sheep shit all over me from out there. Oh, hell, Ruby, there are sheep ghosts."

A quarter mile from the Kelly ranch, they began to re-lease the dogs, one at a time, each one wearing a sheepskin, with holes cut for the head and legs, then tightly sewn to last through several attempts to chew it off. A few drops of high life applied under the tail and the dogs sped for home.

From the rise, the three of them waited as the yelping canines rushed homeward—barking and yapping. A light appeared in the living room and soon several blasts of a shotgun broke the night's silence.

"I can't believe that man is shooting his own dogs." Matty said.

Tad said, bent over in laughter, "But he thinks—they're sheep grazing—his yard."

"He'll learn a lesson from tonight. We better get some sleep," Slocum said. "Who's next on your list?"

"Cy Broyles," Matty said.

"What do we know about him?"

"He's courting a Mormon gal who lives over in Fly Creek."

"Good, he's next."

Under the sliver of a moon Cy reined up the team and climbed out of the buckboard. It was past midnight, and he was making his usual return trip from the Logan homestead and an evening of courting Milicent Durrel. A large, leafy branch had fallen across the road. When he bent over to pick it up, two strong hands grasped his arms and someone jerked a hood down over his head. Unable to see or break loose, he shouted obscenities at his captors, who proceeded to tie his arms and legs. Then they unceremoniously loaded him facedown into a wagon full of sheep.

The sheep were at liberty to step on him, nibble at him when curious, and then defecate on him for the many miles that he was hauled. Sometime near dawn he was dumped equally unceremoniously on the ground near his own wagon and the parties responsible left undetected.

Two nights later Sam Dugan was awakened shortly after midnight by his dogs raising Cain. Unsure what the problem was, he went to the barn to see about the commotion. When he lifted the bar and opened his barn door, ten head of wild yearling steers stampeded, each critter with white rings painted around their eyes and SHEEP spelled out on its sides.

He sat on his butt with hat cocked to the side and cursed his dogs as they chased the animals through a line of drying clothes.

Then the crash of glass followed by a shrill scream came from the house! Sam leaped to his feet and rushed to see what else was wrong.

Matty turned her horse to leave the security of the pines. "Wonder what she screamed so loud for?"

"Danged if I know," Tad chuckled as the three headed out.

"We've got to do something!" Dan Burnett said before he dismounted his horse in front of the Wolf Tongue line shack.

Rafter Sikes, seated in the rocker on the porch, moved his sore leg with some effort and looked up at the assembled ranchers who had just ridden in. He'd been laid up at the Wolf Tongue camp for two weeks, and his leg still hurt.

"They've done it all now," Cy said.

"What's that?"

"They hauled me around in a wagon full of sheep shit all night. They scared Dan Burnett to death with some flying ghost thing up on the Utah road. They painted some wild calves and locked them up in Sam's barn and then they stampeded them. Them yearlings took down his wife's laundry on the line. One of them crazy calves with a corset around its head got so spooked, it jumped through the bedroom window and got on the bed with his wife, Alva.

"And they shook Kelly Blue up so bad that he shot all his dogs for being gawddamn sheep."

"Yeah, and I got home with a sack full of sheep shit instead of Arbuckle coffee," Josh Michaels said.

"They've put sheep pellets in every damn thing. My wife's rain barrel. The pockets of my clothes. I can't see how the hell they done it either."

"Yes, sir," Buster Reines said, "I guess when we was sleeping they climbed in the window and they even put sheep shit in my wife's cedar chest."

"My boys have been out looking for them every day," Rafter said, leaning back in his chair. "I have no idea where they're denned up at. I say we put a bounty on their heads and hire us some gun slicks."

"You boys can do what you want." Sam finally spoke

up from where he sat his horse. "I'm going to arrange me a truce. So we shot a few sheep and now they've had their fun. But I don't call a wild steer shitting in my bed in the middle of the night and busting up the damn furniture funny, but I'll accept that as repayment. I've got the point that little girl made and I'm saying we quit harassing them."

"You ready to give up over something like that?" Rafter demanded.

"Listen"—Sam's dark eyes narrowed—"I've been in these kind of feuds in Texas. No one wins. Her sheep ain't going to hurt no more than the too many cattle we've all got this range stocked up with."

"Too many cattle?" Rafter fumed.

"Yes, too many cattle! Why, you never even sold none of yours this year. Hell, they've eaten everything in sight. We need to make a truce with her. Everyone needs to sit down and agree on how many cattle we can run up here and do it right. Do something before we ain't got diddly left to graze on up here."

"You go sign up with that she-bitch," Rafter swore. "And next year there will be more sheep up here than pine trees. They ever learn you're soft on them woolie boogers, they'll come and come by the billions."

"Sam makes lots of sense. We ain't got any grass left," Cy said.

"Boys, better the cows get it than the winter rot, huh?" Rafter ignored the two. He needed to save his coalition of cattlemen. It was dangerous for men like Sam and Cy to be ready to quit, they could influence others to do the same. "Why, hell, next spring it will be green again all over this country. It does that every year. Overgrazed! Why, shitfire, Sam, you don't know a thing about what you're talking about."

"I'm saying I don't want war. I'll let the rest of you all decide for yourself. Myself, I'm finding that gal and ending my war with her."

"Sam, don't do something foolish. We don't need her sheep up here."

"I don't need trouble with my neighbors. I left Texas because of that, I'm getting too old to rebuild ranches," he said, mounted, ready to leave, and looking back at Rafter. "I know all about overgrazing, it'll bring barb wire next."

"You're crazy, old man. First sum bitch strings that up here is dead!"

"You can't kill them all," Sam said, and rode off.

"Me too," Cy said. "I'm going." He unhitched his horse, looked for a moment at the somber-faced men, and then rode after Dugan.

"Men, ride out now and we can kiss your range goodbye," Rafter said. "It was a little dry this summer. But Sam's full of hot air about that overgrazing business. Ain't no need in that grass being piled up and rotting over the winter. And those sheep, now they'll overgraze it all."

"How we going to stop this ghost-sheep business?" Josh Michaels asked.

"Give me a little time?"

"Not much, my wife is scared to be left alone. Two cowboys already have quit Dan over it. They found dead sheep inside their bedrolls."

"Give me a chance, boys. I'll get it stopped and won't no one be the wiser."

"Maybe we need the law up here."

"What for? We can handle our own business," Rafter said, wondering who had blurted out that dumb idea. All they needed was the law meddling in their affairs. "Everyone, go home. Be on the lookout, we can stop this. I'll find them, I guarantee you."

He sat on the porch until everyone left.

"Ain't there some sheep droppings around that McArthur place?" Rafter asked his youngest son as they watched the ranchers ride out.

"Sure, but what for? Neither that girl, the federal man,

nor the gunman have been near that place. Why, Arland's watched it like a hawk for two weeks.''

''Tonight you slip over there and get me about four big handfuls of it in a poke.'' If they could plant sheep shit, so could he. All around the dead bodies of the traitors in this land.

''What you going to do, Paw?''

''You don't need to know right now, but if we ain't careful, bastards like Sam Dugan are going to let them damn sheepherders in here by the droves.''

15

Snow began to fall, Slocum watched it from the cavern entrance. He drew on the quirlie in the corner of his mouth. Then he slowly inhaled, savoring the smoke and considering what they should do next.

"Can I go see my father?" Matty asked, coming from behind and hugging him by the waist.

"I figure they're watching him close. Don't you?" he asked.

"Yes, the other night we saw that damn Arland Sikes boy was camped there."

"I guess we could hog-tie him." Slocum grinned at the notion as he hugged her shoulder. Their undercover work had been fun to plan and carry out. He wondered what that poor woman thought when she opened her cedar chest and found the sheep pellets.

"Do you think we're winning?"

"We aren't losing. Tad asleep?" he asked, looking back in the cave.

"Tad," she called to him

He rose and began to rub the sleep from his eyes. "What's next?"

"I think he's enjoying this too," Slocum said as they walked back to talk with him.

"We're going to sneak up and hog-tie Arland Sikes," she said, squatting down on her boot heels.

"Sure, I'm game. Let me have some coffee and I'll be ready."

"Matty wants to visit her father and see how he's doing. So I figured we'd kind of slip up Indian-style and grab the lookout."

"Sounds good to me. When do we go?"

"After we all have some of this fresh coffee. Between the darkness and the snowfall, we should have good cover."

"Slocum, how are we going to know if we're winning or not?" Tad asked, busy pulling on his boots.

"Matty, who can we talk to and won't give us out to them?"

"I'm not certain, not after the raid and all."

"What about Mrs. Gray? Would she know anything?"

"Yes, she might," Matty agreed, pouring the coffee.

Single file, they slipped through the pines. The wet snow accumulated on man, beast, and boughs. The steam from their mounts' mouths looked like the product of a teakettle spout. Slocum halted them and Matty secured their horses. The two men began the on-foot part. They located Arland's horse, mantled in snow; he spooked at their approach.

Slocum froze, hand on his gun butt in fear that Sikes might have heard him. They waited in their tracks for a full minute, then stepped over to the pony. With his knife Slocum slit the mohair girth almost in two, then replaced the fender.

Meanwhile Tad took the rifle from the boot, quietly emptied the receiver, and replaced the rounds with powderless ones, tipped with bullets. Slocum had looked all around for any sign of Sikes. He obviously was hiding in a building or some shelter to get out of the snowfall.

It was the unmistakable sound of a cork coming from a whiskey bottle that drew his attention to the open-faced shed. Slocum took Tad by the arm and pointed to the nearby shed. They had nearly walked past him.

The Yale man nodded that he understood. Slocum made a sign that he would go by and distract the man and for Tad to move in.

"Let me go, you're better at taking him," he whispered.

"No, you take him."

Slocum acted like he was going to sneak right by the man. His boots crunching snow, he wondered after all this time how itchy-fingered Sikes would be.

"Hold it right there!" Arland said, and stepped out of the shed.

"Who are you?" Slocum demanded.

"None of your damn business, you sheep-screwing bastard—"

The clunk of Tad's gun butt applied to Arland's head sounded loud. Slocum swept the pistol away from the man as he sprawled facedown into the snow. They dragged him into the shed. His hands tied behind him and a mask pulled down over his face, he sent Tad after the girl. Slocum finished tying his feet with the rope he'd brought.

"Thanks," she said in passing, and hurried for the house.

"He ain't going to give us any more trouble tonight," Tad said as he rubbed his hands together for warmth.

"Not tonight anyway."

"I'm sort of anxious to hear what effect all this has had on them," Tad said softly so the prisoner could not hear if he wasn't out cold and only playing possum.

"It's affected them. We may need to do more, but it's affected them. They know we're out here."

Slocum figured a half hour had passed; Arland had moaned a lot. But with his feet and boots bound, he wasn't going anywhere. The hood effectively kept him from seeing and they were both silent, watching for Matty's return.

She came huddled under a blanket for additional warmth,

white with snow in just the short walk from the house.

"What did you find out?" Tad asked.

"Not here," Slocum said, and tossed his head toward the bound prisoner.

"Let me out of here, you bastards. My paw's going to hang all of you!" Arland shouted.

Matty ran over and kicked him so hard in the leg, he howled, then she did it again.

"There, you worthless piece of shit! Be any hanging done around here, you may be the one dances on that rope, Arland Sikes!"

Slocum caught her arm and they hurried to their mounts in the snow-laden trees.

"How is your father?"

"Doing great, better than I ever hoped for. He's up walking with her help. He's getting stronger too. Still wobbly, but he wanted to come out and help us. He thinks we're doing lots of good from the words he's getting from the store loafers."

"Wonderful, did he know anything else?"

"Yes, Sam Dugan and Cy Broyles have quit Sikes's bunch. Sam sent my father word that he wants to make peace with us."

"When? Where?"

"Anytime, I guess. What are you thinking, Slocum?"

"Night's about gone. It's time we got back and all. We need to plan to go by Sam's place tomorrow night and speak to him."

"You think the war's about over?" she asked as they mounted up.

"Matty, two men don't stop the war, but they could have a good effect on others."

"I'm sure pleased with his progress," she said, looking back toward the house through the curtain of inky white.

"So are we," Tad said.

"Amen," Slocum said.

• • •

Rafter Sikes sat his horse under the wool blanket, Winchester across his lap. The damn snow had set in about sundown. He'd hoped from his vantage point to get a clear shot at Sam Dugan when he came out of the house. If someone didn't stop that sorry Texan from talking his peace bullshit, the others would quit fighting too.

It took just one bad apple in a barrel to spoil the rest. Cy Broyles wouldn't influence many, but lots of men listened to Sam, he was kinda looked up to. A good animal doctor, Sam had saved many a horse or cow from death. That was why he had to be eliminated and the sheep interest blamed for his murder. Both of those factors had to be in play—some evidence of sheepmen doing the shooting. That would rile up everyone, not just the sheep haters. Damn snow was closing in, more coming down by the hour. His leg was simply sore, but the drop in temperature wasn't helping that. He'd have to give up until a better time.

Why hadn't that girl come back home? Was she out of the country? There was talk at the store, the old man was getting better. If McArthur got better, they'd better lay him down too. Those three must be hiding close by, else they couldn't put out the stuff they'd done. His leg kept improving, they'd start really looking for them. By damn, he'd find their hideout and hang the three of them for killing Sam Dugan. He looked with a grin through the fury of the flakes toward the Dugan house; he could see the lamplit windows.

Another night and he'd get him. Rafter raised the reins and turned the horse toward the Wolf Tongue line shack. Arland was on guard duty at the McArthur place. Steven and Ned were out riding every day, trying to find where the three were hiding; not much more they could do.

Naoma should be coming home soon. He needed to go check and see if she was back. Funny thing, the three of them must have buried Barbara when they followed him out; he'd sent the two oldest ones back to the ranch to handle that chore, they'd found a fresh grave, was all, and no corpse.

He pushed the horse out onto the road and booted him into a faster walk. Maybe he'd go by the store and see if there was any more damage done by the three of them. At times it seemed like they were an army, scattered all over the place, leaving things inside folks' houses and spooking them.

Some fool shot a sheep in his yard twenty times one night, and it turned out to be a sheet wrapped around hay to look like one. Everyone was edgy as hell. If he didn't get something going against them, more cattlemen would join Sam and Cy and quit the fight.

This federal man hadn't brought the U.S. marshals in yet either. Maybe he wasn't what they said he was. But he'd acted like a damn agent of some kind.

He dismounted at the hitch rack and went inside.

"You're getting along better on that leg?" someone asked, looking up from a card game under the wagon-wheel lamp overhead.

"Some better. Arland been in here tonight?"

"Yeah, like every evening, he comes by here about dark."

"You got any whiskey left?" he asked the storekeeper.

"Here, try some of this new stuff." Barney put the bottle on the counter. "We just made it this week. Tell me what you think?"

He filled a jigger and waited for Rafter's answer.

The door burst open and Arland staggered inside.

"That sum bitches tricked me and hit me over the head," he said, looking out of his bloodshot eyes at everyone assembled in the store. His clothing was covered with snow, twigs, and dirt.

"Who?"

"That damn federal man and that gunslinger." He leaned against a post, out of breath and shaken.

"She with them?"

"Hell, yes, she nearly broke my damn leg kicking me when I was tied up and down."

"Let's go trail them. I say a hundred apiece reward on them. I'll pay it dead or alive," Rafter said, looking over the crowd.

"Don't get me wrong, Mr. Sikes," Barney began, "but you boys better not go off half cocked. I seen this man you're calling a gunslinger in this very store. He ain't some dumb Mexican or Navaho herder. He's got steel in his veins."

"You telling me that you're too damn chicken to hunt down the bastard?"

"I'm telling you, I've seen that man and I don't want no part of pointing no guns at him, because he'll kill you deader than a dog that fast. It's your war, not mine."

Rafter saw the others wilt. No guts, he didn't need them anyhow. "Come on, Arland, let's go get them."

"I've got to buy me a new cinch first."

"What the hell for?"

"Those bastards cut mine in two, that's why. Dumped me on my ass in the snow and my horse run off. That's why I'm so gawddamn mad!"

Rafter's breath whistled through his nose. He'd like to smother them one at a time with a pillow, so they'd agonize, by damn, some like she did. The way the snow was falling, they'd probably not find a trail anyway.

Rafter looked over at the storekeeper talking under his breath with the cardplayers. He realized that Sam had been twisting Barney's arm to his side. The sum bitch would turn every one in the damn country against him before long. Sam Dugan was a dead sum bitch. His widow better make herself a black dress real quick.

16

"No problems, huh?" Rafter asked himself out loud as he limped across the line shack.

"We've got all kinds of problems. Them sheepherders, they sneak up on your brother, hog-tie him, and cut his cinch. And ain't a man in that store with guts enough to come out and track them down. Sam Dugan has them all thinking those three are the toughest things since Jesse James. We know one is a damn girl and hell, you boys jerked her pants down once. She very tough that day?"

"No, she squalled like a rabbit," Arland said with a big foolish grin.

"Then how come a dumb tenderfoot and one, mind you, one guy they think is a gunfighter would make that whole bunch turn tail on me?"

"Paw—"

"Shut up, I'm doing the talking. There's some tough guys up at Cedar City, the Lonigan brothers. I'm going up there and hire them to plant that damn federal man and the gunfighter."

"How much will they cost?" Steven asked, shocked his father would even consider such an outlay.

"Doesn't matter, we don't stop them three, we'll have every sheepherder in the southwest on this mountain come spring. You've got to show force or they'll run over you."

"We don't even know this gunman's name," Ned said, looking up at the others with a peeved set to his mouth.

"Call him shit, it won't matter when them Lonigan brothers get here. They're tough now, and I mean tough."

"Where you getting this big money?" Arland asked.

"Why, out of our kitty." He gave his eldest a frown. When did he start running the WTS money business?

"What'll we do for supplies?" Arland asked.

"Charge them till spring and we sell cattle."

"Ma told us you had less than four hundred bucks in that kitty."

"What the hell are you getting at?"

"How are you going to hire two killers and have any money left?"

"Your maw didn't know everything in this world. I had more than that. I never told her."

"We been wondering, you're so anxious to get rid of these two, do they know something about Ma's dying?" Arland asked.

"What the hell are you talking about!" he raged, and started across the room.

Arland jumped up and backed to the wall. "You never did say how she died. I just wondered—"

"Your poor maw musta had a stroke and a heart attack in the night. She didn't have no wounds and she was already dead when I found her."

He dropped into the chair and cried in his hands. They would never doubt him again. This was good. From now on it would be the Sikeses against the rest of them—rid of them sheepherders and he could pick off the other ranchers one at a time. He'd have his empire on top of this plateau.

First one he'd eliminate would be Sam Dugan, the over-grazer. He'd show him over grazing on top of his grave.

"You want one of us to go with you, Paw?" Steven asked.

"Where, son?" he asked, drying his eyes on the bandanna.

"Cedar City with you to hire them brothers?"

"No, I'll go. You boys keep looking for them. They've got to be somewhere out there. You get them, we save the bounty. All right?"

"Snow's getting bad. We get much more, we could be locked in," Ned said.

"So will they."

"Yeah, I know, but they know where we are," Ned said.

"You getting squeamish, Ned?"

"Stealing a few strays in Utah and moving them south ain't bad business. But killing people could get plenty of law up here."

"We ain't killing them, Ned." He shook his head in disgust.

"What if they prove we hired these guys or they squeal on us?"

"What if the damn sky falls in?"

"It might, and we're all taking a helluva risk doing this with you."

"You want out, Ned?" He pointed to the door. "Just leave now!"

"No." Ned turned the other way.

"Then shut up and do your part."

Slocum drew a deep breath and watched the snow pile up in front of the cave. He had talked about moving over to Lee's Ferry and wintering with the sheep. They had made one fast trip there and back for supplies. The Navaho boys had the herd in hand, were training new dogs, and by the final count they'd lost only a hundred head. Some had died afterward from their bullet wounds, but the flock was settled and doing well.

As private a man as John Lee was, he was not likely to

tell Sikes and them much. He had little to say and acted to Slocum like a man with a past. There had been rumors for years he had been the one who led the Mormon raid on the California-bound Arkansas wagon train in southern Utah. It was supposed to look like Indians had done it. Killed all the grown-ups, took the kids and parceled them out. The raiders divided the spoils, a huge herd of cattle, horses, oxen, and a large sum of money.

"This snow continues, what's going to happen?" Tad asked.

"Those folks have stock and no hay to feed will lose their herd. They won't care if sheep come or not."

"What about House Rock?"

"Most folks say it stays clear. Several cows were down there, did you notice?"

"I saw some when we rode over to the ferry."

"There's quite a few cattle in the valley. There's several different brands down there. But I didn't see many WTS cattle, I think the bulk of them are still on the mountain."

"I don't understand?" Tad frowned.

"I think that the Sikeses are so obsessed with this business of eliminating the McArthurs that they had given up ranching."

"What will happen?" Tad asked.

"Winter kill," she said, joining them. "Only so much snow an old cow can paw through and find grass, then she huddles up and starves."

"Cruel way to die."

"The shape that these cattle are in and no grass under the snow in lots of places—it'll be a hider's winter," Slocum agreed.

"Hider's winter?"

"Yeah, cowboys out of work, they skin out the dead ones for the hide to make enough money to get by."

"Whew, that sounds like a rough way to live."

"It was. I've had to do it before," Slocum said, and studied the snowfall from his dry position inside the mouth of the cave. "It sure ain't easy. I'd have gave my chair in hell for this cave to live in. We had an old frame shack with cracks this wide between every board." He held his fingers apart to show the width.

Tad shook his head, impressed by the notion.

"Come dark, we're going to slip down and talk to this Sam Dugan," Slocum said, and they both agreed with a nod.

He watched Matty cross the cave floor for the coffeepot. The divided skirt swished around her legs as she walked. There had been no chance for the two of them to be intimate or have any time to themselves since they'd recovered Tad. It was on Slocum's mind, and he knew from little things she did that it was on hers as well.

In the evening, they saddled up. The snow had slacked to a fine spray that melted on contact with Slocum's face. Much came from the pine boughs and sifted down by the night wind. As usual, they made a wide circuit so anyone tracking them would think they were coming from a different direction.

He was eager to talk to Dugan about Sikes. If they could isolate Sikes and his boys from the others, then they could bring the problem to a head. But if they had to fight everyone else, they'd lose.

The bay horse from Sikes's bunch that Slocum rode was handy and surefooted. But Tad had the best mount, a big sorrel. Slocum could imagine how old man Sikes would grit his teeth every time if he knew some tenderfoot had his powerful horse. Matty rode a solid dun, partial payment for shooting their mounts and the trouble Sikes had caused.

They crossed a ridge and came through the dark timber with her leading the way.

"Dugan's place is about four miles south," she said when they stopped to organize. "He has some hay fields, pole-fenced. Remember, it's where we put the wild yearlings in the barn and when he opened the door, they ran over him."

"Yes. You know much about him?"

"Nope, he's a Texan and kinda high-handed. But Daddy said he had quit the Sikeses and sent word that he wanted to talk peace."

"Good." Slocum rose in the stirrups and stretched his tight back muscles. Be nice to be in a warm cabin somewhere, in a real bed, yes, with her, instead of out in the deepening cold night with his toes nearly frozen in the stirrups and facing a confrontation with a man who might not be all that glad to see them.

He booted the bay on.

17

"That new cinch on your saddle good?" Rafter asked his eldest.

"Yeah, where are you heading?"

"On business. No need for you to go back to the McArthurs. Hell, they know you're there and my girth has some broken strands. I'll just use your saddle tonight."

"Go ahead," Arland said, and turned back to the card game the three of them were playing. "I'd like to bust in both their heads for hitting me." He touched the top of his head tenderly. "It still hurts. So's my leg where that bitch kicked me. The nerve of her."

Rafter saved his words. If Arland had been vigilant, he'd never been jumped by those three. Let their old daddy have a chance, he'd eliminate the three of them in short order. Where in the hell could they be hiding so good to be swallowed up? Maybe someone was hiding them at their place. One of the other ranchers—he hadn't seen anything out of place at Dugan's.

The fine snow stuck on his face as he packed Arland's saddle out to the corral. Best horses they had were still

down at the ranch. Those three had probably helped themselves to them. He captured a mount and saddled it quickly.
It would be cold watching the Dugan place this night. Then
he recalled the small poke full of sheep pellets in his own
saddlebags and went after it. He also located two bottles of
whiskey. Too many things to think about. He intended to
pour the shit over Dugan's body, like they'd done in other
places. A marker, he smiled to himself and mounted up,
feeling for the long gun in the scabbard of his borrowed
rig. It was there. He put spurs to the gelding and burst out
into the night.

He'd go after the Lonigan brothers in a day or two. He
wanted Sam's killing to settle in on the folks. They might
get so mad they'd rush out, find those three, and hang them
at no cost to him. He reached into the saddlebag and jerked
out a bottle. The goosy horse under him jumped ahead and
he sawed him down.

"Easy, sum bitch. I need me a little blood warmer here."
He hoisted the bottle to his lips and chugged down some
deep drafts. Finished, he made a loud "aw" and stuck the
bottle back in. Be a good night, he would get a chance to
kill that damn Dugan and half his troubles on this mountain
would be over.

Come springtime, he and the boys would make a round
trip up into Utah and bring back enough cattle to clear up
his debts. By fall the brands would be healed and he could
sell them down at Prescott and no one would be the wiser.
By that time he would have Naoma living at the ranch
house too. He ducked a snow-laden limb and rode up
through darkness of the timber. Come springtime, he'd
have a lot of things straight. Starting this night with Sam
Dugan's demise.

He held the horse back and studied the pearl-white fields.
No need to hurry, he would watch Dugan's place for a
while. He removed the Winchester and checked; there was
a shell in the chamber. Arland had been ready for action.

Loaded to the gate, he slid it back. Sam Dugan was as good as dead.

Slocum dropped off his horse and patted the stock dog that came bouncing out, barking.

"Who's out there?" a man's voice asked. The light in the house went out.

"Friends," Slocum said.

"It's me, Sam Dugan, Matty McArthur," she said, and hurried past Slocum.

"Who's with you?"

"Friends, and we come to talk peace," she said, hesitating a few steps from the darkened porch where Slocum surmised Sam held a gun on them.

"Sam," a woman's voice said. "She's a girl, for Christ's sake, don't shoot her."

"I ain't shooting anyone. I'm just being careful."

"Well, are you going to let them stand out in the cold and let all the heat out of the house too?" she demanded. The sound of the front door shutting at his back drew Slocum's lips into a smile.

"We've come to talk," Matty said.

"I'm listening."

"We want to live and let live. I lost a hundred sheep in the raid and Rafter Sikes came within inches of killing all three of us. Our war isn't with you. I guess I'm saying it must be with Sikes."

"Which one of you has been east of the house three nights now watching my place?" he asked.

"What?" Matty asked, and looked back at Slocum for the answer.

"It hasn't been us, Dugan."

"I went looking for the milk cow two days ago and found in the snow where someone sat on a horse out there for a long time. Checked on it again and they'd came back. I figured it was you three fixing to tree me again."

"No, we're like you, we want the trouble over. If someone is watching you, it has to be one of the Sikes bunch,'' Slocum said, considering the implication of his accusation.

"That could be too. They weren't happy when I pulled out.''

"Who else wants peace?'' Slocum asked.

"Cy Broyles, for one. You all come on inside, sorry I'm sort of edgy about all this.''

"Don't blame you,'' Slocum said with a good look around the starlit yard. He followed Matty inside with Tad on his heels.

"I guess you're the gunfighter they talk about,'' he said, extending his hand.

"That's Slocum and this is Tad Markum.'' Matty introduced them around and they shook hands.

"Have a seat,'' Dugan said, indicating the sofa and some chairs his wife had brought in.

"This is my wife, Myra,'' he said. Both men doffed their hats for the tall, gray-haired woman with an ample chest.

"I'm making some coffee for you all,'' she announced.

"Thanks,'' Slocum said, grateful for the warmth of the room.

"Keeping a blanket over the east window so whoever is out there can't see much.''

"Good idea. Do you think he's out there tonight?'' Slocum asked.

"Been there three nights in a row.''

"We may try some diversion on him,'' Slocum said, taking a steaming coffee cup from the woman. "Why would someone besides us be watching you?''

"I think Sikes is concerned that our parting company might convince others to do the same.''

"We don't want all the range up here,'' Matty said. "Why is everyone worried about five hundred sheep?''

"They think if we let you stay, then the big outfits may come in here and run over them.'' Sam shook his head and loaded his pipe. "I've been in one feud that broke a county up in Texas. I came here for peace and hoped to spend out my years doing what I want, raise cattle, but all that has changed."

"I'm going to stay," Matty said.

"You don't have to convince me. Take your notions to the others. I won't raise a finger to stop you ever again."

"Thanks, you won't regret it. I want all of you to go on talking in here," Slocum said. "I'm slipping outside and going to try and learn who that horse man is."

"Be careful," Matty said so fast, she looked as if she might have regretted her quickness.

Slocum nodded that he had heard her concern. He gave the others a wave and shook his head at Tad, ready to join him, then buttoned up his duster and stepped outside on the porch. To run north to the barn would be a dead giveaway. He moved south from the house to the corrals, where his movements might not be so obvious. He ran low along the side of the pole pens, stopping occasionally and trying to spot the stalker. The skin crawled on the back of his neck as he remembered how they had almost ridden into a trap. They should have scouted around better. Sikes was out for blood, and he no doubt wanted any defector dead too.

But he knew he needed to locate and capture the sentry sitting out there on horseback and ask him some questions. He paused to catch his breath and studied the area that Dugan had indicated east of the house. Then the snort of a horse gave the man's position away—under some low boughs in the tall timber.

Slocum got low and drew out his Colt. He needed some time to get behind the man on horseback unseen. He could tell nothing except someone sat a horse in the timber almost a quarter mile from his position.

An owl swooped low, his shadow skimming the white spans between them. Then a rabbit's scream split the night and the sharp flap of the owl's wings with his prey in his talons sounded as Slocum paused. He did not want to scare the bird of prey and warn the gunman.

The bird, standing on his victim, tore fur and flesh from

the suffering hare until finally a sharp peck silenced his tortured prey. Then the owl stalked around his victim in the starlight. With his wings raised shoulder high, as if hovering over the carcass, he snatched mouthfuls with little regard for the source. His powerful beak crushed bones and he inhaled them.

The owl's soft *hoos* breaking the stillness, Slocum waited on one knee, the cold from the snow seeping through his trousers. He finally moved, hoping the man was too intent on the bird's activities or the house to notice him.

When he reached the timber his heart pounded. His back against a tree trunk, he tried to control his breathing. He was getting closer. The flap of wings meant the owl had finished his supper. How far away was the lookout?

He saw the glint of a gun barrel. The man had a rifle pointed at the house as he sat the horse.

"Drop the gun!" he shouted, and then ducked, hoping to distract the shooter.

The rifle made a snap. A dud, Slocum thought as he came up from the snow to fire his Colt before the man could reload. Distance and all considered, he knew his usual accuracy would be impossible.

The rifle popped on a dud again and that drew a string of curse words. Then the man spanked the horse on the butt and surged away into the timber.

"Hold it!" Slocum shouted, and fired away into the inky night, hoping for some stray lead to stop the retreating gunman. He raced through the snow to the spot where the man had been. On the white ground he saw a cartridge and that the lead was still on the bullet. He shook it and grimaced. The shell had no powder. It was one that he and Tad had fixed to load Arland's gun.

It had not been Arland's voice from the night before. It was Rafter Sikes himself cursing in the night—damn, he'd missed him by seconds. But if the bullets had been good, was he intent on shooting into Dugan's house? It damn sure looked that way.

"Slocum? Slocum? Are you all right?" Matty shouted, coming across the open field of snow.

"I'm fine," he said, sweeping her up in his arms and kissing her quickly.

"Thank God," she said, and buried her face in his chest and hugged him. "Who was it?"

"Rafter Sikes himself, I think."

"Good to see you made it," Tad said, joining them with his pistol in hand. "Did you get him?"

"No, but he was fixing to shoot up the house with our ammo." He handed Tad the cartridge. "Recognize this one?"

"Damn, I put that in Arland's rifle last night."

"What's that?" Sam asked.

"Oh, last night," Tad explained, "we reloaded Arland Sikes's rifle with this ammunition that didn't have any gunpowder in it."

"How come he used that?" Sam scoffed. "Any idiot could feel the weight and tell when he tried to load it."

"We reloaded his gun for him," Tad said.

"I see, and thanks, Slocum. You sure tried to catch him in the act," Sam said. "I'm riding to tell the rest of my neighbors." He held up the bullet. "That one was meant to silence me. I won't forget it, that's for sure."

"Sam," Slocum said.

"Yes?"

"You be on your guard. He's liable to try to back-shoot you anytime."

"I know, come on into the house. Myra has some apple pie for all of us."

18

"Your damn rifle was full of duds!" Rafter shook the long gun in his son's face as he sat up on his elbows in the bunk. "Every shell in there was a dud! Tell me! Am I fighting these stinking sheep lovers by myself? Tonight them three were making deals with Dugan at his house."

"Paw, I swear they must have changed the ammo in that gun. I just checked it the other day."

"I say everyone get up and check their ammo. Pistols, rifles, everything we own. Those bastards were up there and now Sam knows someone was watching him. I'll be gawd-damned!" He slammed the rifle down on the wooden table and sent cups flying. "Come morning, I'm riding up to Utah and hire the Lonigan brothers."

"If we can't get them, how will the Lonigans ever do it?" Ned demanded, busy ejecting the shells from his Colt on the table.

"Because they are real killers, that's why, and you boys ain't shit for nothing!"

"You had that sum bitch in the smoke house and he got away," Arland said.

"Your stupid mother turned him loose was the reason why he got away."

"You never told us that," Steven said.

"How else would that dumb dude get out of there?"

"Why you figure she did that?"

"Mumbled something about them hanging twelve men once in Tennessee to get the right one when she was a girl after someone killed a federal tax man. She didn't want us hung, I guess."

"Yeah," Steven agreed, "didn't want us hung. She was worried about us all the time."

Rafter could feel the his sons' eyes on him. He'd slipped and nearly said too much, mentioning Barb again was stupid. She was dead and buried. Nothing anyone could prove about him and her death could be pinned on him.

"I'm going to Utah in the morning."

"Paw, we need some horse hay," Steven said, concerned.

"Go buy some off one of them polygamous bastards."

"What'll I use for money?"

"Here," he said, giving the boy twenty dollars. "You boys cut some wood while I'm gone too. Damn winter may be a fright."

"We going back to the ranch soon?" Arland asked. "This old shack is cold as hell."

"Yes, we need to. You boys can take the hay you buy back there, trail the horses home and get it all ready, and I'll be back in a few days. Then you can put some of the horses that we don't need over into House Rock until spring."

"Where in the hell is your old sorrel?" Arland asked with a frown.

"That damn dude's riding him."

None of the boys laughed out loud, but their snickers were as bad.

"We're sure going to lose a lot of stock," Steven finally said.

"Can't be helped. I'll bet we find plenty of replacements next spring up in Utah. Right, boys?"

"Yeah."

Wolf Tongue line shack—Slocum had a map from the night before that Sam Dugan had sketched for him, showing how to reach the Sikeses' other place. It was a simple tracing on brown paper. Slocum was sure at this point that the only way to solve their problems was to capture all of them and send them to Prescott bound and tied and deliver them to the law. Maybe Matty was right, they would buy their way out of the charges, but they themselves would have to do that too. He could make certain that their pockets were empty when they got there; maybe that would make a difference.

"We going there in the daylight?" Matty asked.

"Yes, they probably won't expect us then."

"Good, let's go." She grabbed her saddle by the horn and he caught her arm before she could toss it on the dun.

"Why don't you go see about your father in Joseph's Lake? Tad and I can handle them."

"No way, I'm not missing out on this part for nothing."

"Think on it, will you?" He worried about her getting in the line of fire. The dude would make it, either out of his ego or ignorance of the Sikeses' real threat; he was spoiling for a fight. But her, he wished she would listen.

"I'd say you lost that one," Tad said under his breath when Slocum brushed by him.

"You lose every time arguing with women," Slocum said, and used his left hand to toss on the pad, then he lifted the saddle off the ground in his right hand.

Three hours later they rode off the ridge and kept to the timber. Several thin cows were out in the snowy meadows. Their noses peeled and bloody from rooting in the ice and snow for forage, they bawled hungrily.

"Pretty sad sight," she said as they rode on.

"A sign the man has lost his good sense. They should

have been drove off this plateau weeks ago and they'd been saved.''

"Is it too late?" Tad asked.

"They ain't our cows, not one damn thing we can do about it," Slocum said, and shook his head; he never could stand to see an animal suffer.

"Strange things happen out here," Tad said, and booted his horse to get alongside Slocum. "What are we doing with them besides Matty kicking hell out of them and me beating them up when she gets through?"

"Take them prisoners and prefer charges. Kidnapping you, attempted murder, threatening her, shooting up her herd. I'll bet we can find a few more charges. Don't you think so?"

"Damn right!" Tad narrowed his eyes as he stepped aboard and then sat upright in the saddle. "I'm ready for this to be over."

"Boys, I'll be back at the ranch in ten days." Rafter told them. "Get the hay and I'll see you at home." He wanted to add he'd be back with their new mother, but he wasn't certain how that would go over. If Steve was right and those other two had been going over and drilling her too, he had some adjustments to make. He wasn't planning on sharing her with the likes of them.

No matter, he intended to bring his new bride home with him. He wasn't getting any younger, and with the Lonigan boys after the federal man and the gunfighter—hell, they ought to kill that dude for less than the other one, he was so inexperienced. Them gone, his life would be uncomplicated again.

He turned up his collar and faced the north wind on the porch. It would take three days to get to Naoma—a long ride. The horse he rode was sound and surefooted, but the fastest pace would be a trot in the shallower snow.

•   •   •

Slocum studied the unpainted frame structure, weathered gray with a crooked tin stovepipe sticking out of the shingle roof patched with tin cans. Seeing no smoke from the chimney made him pound the fork of his saddle with his palm.

"What are you thinking?" Tad asked.

"No smoke, they've left here and we've missed them."

"Corrals are empty too," Matty pointed out.

"Damn, we've sure rode a long way for the fun of it." Tad laughed.

"Guess we better camp here tonight," Slocum said, checking the low sun. "Tomorrow we can follow tracks."

"Yeah," Tad said, dismounting heavily to lead his horse on in. "We're late again."

"I sure hope they've left some food," she said. "Slocum's jerky is hard on my teeth."

They were soon all three laughing as the long red rays of sun speared across the huge flat meadow that spread like a white sheet around them. The suffering cows bawling was the only part that Slocum hated, they'd catch up with the Sikeses—eventually.

In the cupboard Matty found flour, baking soda, lard, even tomatoes.

"Is there a calf or yearling out there ain't shrunk up that you can cut some tender loins off of?" she asked.

"I'll go get one," Slocum said, confident that he could find what she wanted.

"Guess I get to split and cut wood," Tad said, and picked up the ax.

Slocum returned in an hour with a mess of meat. She took it from him and he washed up on the porch. Twilight had settled on the snowy clearing. One rider's tracks had gone north, three others and the horses had headed east. They must have barely missed them somehow during the day.

"Nice to have your own butcher shop out here," Tad said.

"And you always want to be sure to eat the other guy's

beef and not get caught at it.'' Slocum laughed with him as he dried his hands. ''I've ridden for some big outfits, and they considered it a shame to have to eat a calf bearing their brand.

''Made some big cattle drives up to Kansas. We had to ride through three thousand cattle to find one didn't have our trail brand on it for the cook to butcher each time.''

''Why are you out here with no visible means of support?'' Tad asked, looking toward the black outline of the forest.

''Drifting,'' Slocum said.

''You don't own any real estate, no home, no wife?''

''None of those things,'' Slocum said. ''I get kind of itchy pinned down too long. What about you?''

''Me? I'd love to own all this country. Have a nice home. Lots of livestock, hunt some of this game out here, like the big mule deer we've seen, get another lion and an elk too.''

''Pick you a spot and go to it,'' Slocum said.

''That doesn't interest you in the least, does it?''

Slocum offered him a cigar from his pocket, and when Tad refused, he bit the end off it and stuck it in his mouth. He scratched a lucifer to life and drew deep.

''Might be nice back here if no one came by for five or ten years.''

''I mean an economic enterprise. There's good timber here and probably minerals besides the grazing. If there was a way to get a railroad in here—''

''How are you getting it over the Grand Canyon?'' Slocum frowned in disbelief at his wild imagination.

''There's a way or there will be one.''

''You two are going to freeze out there. Come inside and drink my coffee,'' she said, hugging herself for warmth.

''Hell, Matty, Tad and I been making fortunes out here,'' Slocum said, noticing that his face reddened at the remark.

''Good, did you get rid of Sikes in the meanwhile?''

''Yeah, we stampeded them off into the Colorado gorge.''

"Good riddance," she said, and set a bottle of whiskey on the table.

"Figured you two could use a good snort. They had that real well hid out. Never would have found it, but I discovered the trunk they kept things in had a false bottom."

"We'll drink to our success," Slocum said, and Tad agreed.

They sat back in the ladderback chairs while the meat sizzled in the pan and toasted prosperity, sipping the raw whiskey from tin cups. Then Slocum remembered his horse was unsaddled and went to take care of it.

His soles crunched on the snow as he fed corn to the three horses from the near-empty granary. His saddle on a rack in the shed beside theirs, he eyed the area as a place to spread his bedroll. Snow free, he decided he would sleep out there on the old hay.

Long after they had turned in, he lay with his head on the saddle in the open front shed and listened to the night noises. He heard light footsteps and watched in the starlight as she came around the corner of the line shack. She looked back over her shoulder as she tiptoed inside the shed. Wrapped in a blanket, she looked like a ghostly form.

He pretended to be asleep when she knelt down and kissed him on the mouth. Then his arms reached out and she gave a start and a yip.

"Shush, he'll hear you," he said, amused as he threw back the covers and she slipped beneath them with him.

"He wouldn't hear a freight train," she said, shedding her long-tailed shirt and then pressing her cool flesh to his.

"You sure?" he asked, drawing in a deep breath for his own strength. Her presence quickly ignited his senses when he realized she was stark naked.

"Slocum, believe me, that boy is sleeping one off."

"Good." He raised her chin up and then kissed her.

Her firm breasts nested against him, she sprawled on his chest, and he kneaded the muscles in her back and butt. She melted in his arms as they lusted in each other's closeness, tasting and retasting, rock-hard nipples, hungry mouths. They were alone in a faraway land. He finally moved on top of her and plunged into the center of passion's volcano.

The sound of her sharp cries of pleasure were like the killdeer's song. She moaned and clung to him as they soared higher and higher until finally the bomb inside their brains exploded and they drifted back down like an autumn leaf—and settled dreamily in each other's arms. Spent and dizzy, they savored being one in a warm niche as cold air seeped in to cool their hot bare skin.

19

Cedar City basked in the warmer sun. Rafter dismounted at the livery and handed the boy his reins.

"Be twenty cents if you want grain," the swamper said. A boy of about fifteen waited while Rafter dug out the money. All the time he searched for the change, his mind was busy recalling Naoma's sister's husband's name.

"You ever heard of someone named Ames. I think Delbert Ames is the man's name."

"There's an Ames lives up the road in the first green house." The ragged-clothed boy pointed up the hill.

"Good, and take care of the horse," he said, and left the boy.

The wooden boardwalk was the only place not muddy from the melted precipitation. Rafter hiked uphill on it until he reached the green frame house the boy had mentioned. He disregarded his appearance; after all, he'd been on the sloppy road for three days with no place to clean up—while he was mud-caked and disheveled, he was also damn eager to see Naoma.

A woman in her fifties came to the door and scowled at

him worse than Barbara ever did. He removed his hat.

"Beggars go to the back door," she said, and started to close it.

"Ma'am," he said, forcing it to stay open with both his hands, "I'm not here on no damn begging mission."

"Then what do you want?" she asked haughtily.

"This is the Delbert Ames house, isn't it?"

"One of them." She drew her shoulder farther back.

"Oh, I want the one where Mrs. Naoma Worthen is staying at."

The woman shook her head. "She certainly isn't here."

"Dammit, lady, where is she?" He was fast growing peeved at this old snooty sister.

"At one of his other houses!"

"Good, give me the directions."

"Two blocks up and one to the right. Third one on the right."

"Wait." He again stopped her from closing the door. "What color is it?"

"Why, green, of course, All my husband's houses are green."

"Gawd damn. I mean, excuse me. How many houses does he have?"

"Five. Now, get away."

"Thank you," he said, backing up and bowing with his hat in his hand.

Damn, this town living was something else. Walk here and walk there, a man could wear out a pair of soles doing all this walking. If he was Delbert and married to that old battle-ax, he'd spend all his time with the pretty ones. One thing for sure, this Delbert must do quite well—five green-painted houses and some gal and a family in each one of them. These old polygamists must be some kinda stud horses, a gal in every house and only seven days in a week. Whew, wonder what he was like?

He finally reached the frame house, which was smaller than the first but the only green one on the block. He knocked on the door and a woman with a baby at her breast answered.

"Yes, sir?"

"Ma'am, I'm looking for—"

"Rafter, darling!" Naoma screamed, and ran across the room to hug him. "My goodness, you do smell like an old horse," she said, straightening up and taking him by the hand inside and closing the door behind him.

"Well, I'm sorry, darling, I never—"

"We can fix that. Take off your clothes," she said. She undid his gun belt and rolled it around the holster.

"Here. What about her?" He gulped big-time.

"Rachel's seen men before. My gosh, that's her third baby."

"I'll go put the water on so he can bathe," Rachel said, and left with the newborn holding tight to her elongated pink nipple.

"My goodness, it is sure good to see you. How have things been going?"

"Well, Barbara died," he said as she unfastened and peeled away his clothing.

"She did. I mean, she did?"

"Had a stroke in the night."

"That's sad. There you are," she said as she finished removing his long handles. "I'll wash these for you."

He acknowledged her offer as he hugged himself, standing naked in the living room of the small house. Feeling like a great peeled onion, he wondered if he should cover himself with his hands when Rachel came back. He sure was shriveled up in this cool room. Naoma went and found him a blanket to wear while he waited for the water to heat and then she gave him a sly grin.

"I'm sure glad business brought you up here," she said.

"Oh, yeah." He did have business; he needed to find the Lonigan brothers. He'd gotten so excited about finding her, he had almost forgotten his true mission. She sure looked good. The dress she wore was kind of plain, but he knew how her short legs looked like sausages and her soft belly was great to lay on and her full breasts were the best of all. Big things come in a small package, yes, sir.

"Come on," she said, taking him by the arm. "Rachel said your bathwater is ready."

He swallowed hard, wondering if both of them were giving him a bath. Rachel smiled at him, the sleeping baby all wrapped up in a shawl as she went by him. Then Naoma led him into the kitchen. He held on to the blanket, feeling like a calf being led to slaughter.

The tub looked inviting. It was a big oval copper one with a high back, and a quick look at the steaming water made him suck in his gut. He tested the temperature with one foot. A little hot, but not bad, he began to lower himself slowly in, when Rachel came back into the room, pushing the sleeves up on her robe and he could see this was to be a three-party bath. His breathing came a little short as he got as deep as he could in the hot water: the two sisters on their knees, one on each side, began to scrub his broad, hairy chest with lye soap. His arms were next and then his head. A bucket of rinse water left him drenched, but they worked with vigor, laughing and discussing him as they went.

"I bet you never been this clean before?" Naoma asked.

"No, I ain't," he agreed. Rachel smiled at him and soaped up a brush. He sure hoped she didn't plan to dive in with that and wash his privates like they had the rest of his body. He held his breath when she stuck it under the water and he nearly rose out of the tub when she got close to scrubbing the inside of his leg.

"Ain't this fun?" Naoma asked.

"Lots of fun," he agreed, deciding Rachel was a turn on the thinner side than her sister, but a nice-looking gal of about twenty-five, he guessed. He never was certain, he thought Naoma was thirty-two, but she could have been forty. He froze when a hand closed on his shaft under the water.

He looked at one sister, then the other. Rachel wrinkled her nose. She had him.

"You can have him first," she finally said to Naoma. Then she let go and he drew in a copious volume of air.

After she dressed him in a robe that must have belonged to Delbert, Naoma led him into the shade-darkened bedroom and she began to undress.

"What's wrong, Rafter, honey? Ain't you pleased to be here?" she asked.

He swallowed hard and barely managed to get out from his restricted throat, "When's her husband coming home?"

"Not until next Tuesday."

"What day of the week is this?" he gasped.

"Wednesday."

He closed his eyes as he undid the belt on the robe and shook his head in disbelief. This was Wednesday and her husband didn't come home until next week. My, my, with his rod hardening as he crawled on the bed, he wondered how many ways one could do it. He might just learn.

Slocum saddled their horses. The smell of beef back strap frying made him smile. Tad was a mite hung over. He had stood around in the line shack and sipped coffee without a word or even a question. A certain sign he was either sick or in bad shape. Bedrolls tied down, Slocum went inside for breakfast. They were going to find the boys first. That was the plan, they'd ride by Joseph's Lake and get some supplies. Sam should have things settled down and she could go up and check on her daddy while they were there.

"Damn, Slocum, was there a mule in that bottle?" Tad asked, holding the back of his head.

"No, just good liquor."

"Whew, I'm out of it today."

"I just hope he can hang on to the saddle horn and ride," Matty teased.

"Well," Tad said with a weary shake of his head. "I'm

going to try. Don't clang another pan though, please, Matty?''

"You'll get better in a week," Slocum promised him, with a wink for Matty.

"Oh, yes, in ten days you'll be over half the headache."

"Come on, you two, this is bad enough."

They both laughed at Tad's expense, and as if that wasn't enough, halfway through breakfast he rushed outside and lost it all.

She reached over, and with Tad out of sight, squeezed Slocum's arm. "I told you he was out of it last night."

He agreed with a smile.

Barney McKey came out on the porch when they rode up to his Joseph's Lake store. Several of the loafers joined him. Slocum swung his Colt around in a handy position. They looked friendly, but he took no chances.

"I guess all of us owe the two of you an apology. And you too, big fellow from Yale, but you come asking for it." Then he shook his head. "Sam Dugan has sent word to have a deputy and a judge come up here. We're all planning on pleading guilty to disturbing the peace, paying our fine, as well as replacing your wagon, supplies, and the sheep that you lost, ma'am."

"That's mighty fine of everyone, Barney, but it's more serious than that," Matty said.

Slocum watched her and listened. She didn't have to do this, expose herself to public ridicule and a trial. He wanted to stop her.

"Sam told us," Barney interceded, "how the Sikeses tried to kill the Yale man and you two as well. And how he would have killed Sam and Myra if it hadn't been for you all. The man's crazy. The law will take care of him."

She wet her lips and nodded, not looking up.

Slocum rode in close and spoke softly but sharply. "That's enough. Let's get our supplies. The law will handle them now."

"I just couldn't tell them," she said, and tears began to run down her cheeks. "I just couldn't tell them—"

Slocum stripped off his kerchief and shoved it in her hands. "Here, why don't you and Tad go up and see your daddy. Meantime, I'll get the supplies. We can stop worrying about the Sikeses. The law will handle them from here on."

Tad was by her other stirrup. "Come on, sounds like we won, Matty."

"I know, I just can't believe it is all." She dove off into Slocum's arms and her tears soon soaked his shirt. She hugged Tad too when he came around to her side of the horse.

"You two saved me," she sobbed. "You did. I never would have fought them without the two of you."

"Take her up to her father's and let him know if he doesn't already know. I'll get those supplies and then we'll go to Lee's Ferry and check on the Navahos and the sheep."

"That can wait. Come up to the place, both of you," she said. Her eyes flooded with tears, the traces streaked down her flush face. "We can go check on the sheep in the morning."

The moon had risen, barely a sliver. Slocum stood in the barn doorway and pulled on his fresh quirlie, the red glow lighting his face as he smoked. He was still a week away from Prescott, maybe longer. He might cut south at the Little Colorado crossing.

He watched her slip from the dark house, then go from tree shadow to tree. A shiver of excitement ran up his spine. He sent the cigar butt spiraling in a great red arc.

"I saw your match," she said, and hugged him.

"You could catch a death of cold out here," he said, realizing she wore only a thin robe.

"Good, then you save me. Take me to your warm bed." She looked up in his eyes and grinned.

"Matty, you know I can't stay here much longer."

"I figured some damn hounds were after you the first day you came." She hugged his waist and rested the side of her face on his chest. "I knew I'd never fall for no ordinary guy. Slocum, dammit, I knew it all the time, but I didn't want to admit it to myself. I wanted you to be afoot forever and to drive my sheep wagon wherever I needed it driven and be here when I needed you. Like right now."

"I ain't passing you on, but that Yale man has lots of bottom."

"Don't bust my dream. Tad will be here, I'm sure, whenever I get over you."

"Do that, get over me. Say, it's cold out here."

"I thought you'd never ask me."

She halfway shoved him inside. He looked back at the thin moon. He'd need to get moving; it was probably past time. He toed off his boots and watched her lift up the blankets and then get under them.

Somewhere there was warm, snug cabin with a roaring juniper logs in the fireplace radiating out more heat than the sun, and a large Navaho blanket on the floor to sprawl on top of in the warmth. A place to hold her up and kiss her bare shoulders and nipples and navel and the tender insides of her legs until she couldn't stand it anymore. Then ride the ocean until they crashed on the craggy shore. He closed his eyes as he held her and began his campaign, the smooth skin of her shoulders under his hot, demanding mouth.

20

Cedar City after dark was a murky place to find his way. Rafter had left the two women for the first time in three days. His lower back ached, his bad leg was sore, and at first he wasn't sure he could walk three blocks. He had to find the Lonigan brothers and make it quick. This might be a Mormon town, but folks operated saloons for the jack Mormons, the ones who drank despite the church's staunch stand against alcohol, and those the Mormons called outsiders, the Gentiles.

He found the Red Horse and entered the smoky room. A noisy pool game was going on, the participants loud as they crowded the rectangular table, giving the shooter advice. He slipped to the bar and ordered a beer. He didn't need to get drunk, he had some tough business to handle with these men if they were around.

" 'Evening," the barkeep said, and waited for Rafter's order.

"A beer and some information?"

"Beer's a dime. Most information is free." The man smiled behind his handlebar mustache.

"I need to talk to the Lonigan brothers."

The man heard him, he could tell he was digesting the notion. Finally he pursed his lips and spoke softly.

"They don't like to be disturbed."

"When's a good time to see them?"

"Like never. They play poker or they, well, sleep. Unless they're out of town on business."

"That's why I'm here," he said, and looked around to be sure no one was close enough to hear him. "I want to hire them."

"Oh, that's different. I'll get your beer. Then I'll go see when they've got time to see you. What's your name?"

"Rafter Sikes, from Joseph's Lake," he said to the man, who then left. He looked up at the naked woman reclining on some clouds in the mural behind the bar. Two or three other nudes graced the walls, but the heavy smoke obscured most of them.

"Here's the beer, Mr. Sikes, it's a dime."

Rafter paid the man. His three-day orgy with the two sisters had left him shaken and even somewhat disoriented. He wasn't too certain if it was day or night. He had amazed himself at his own stamina, but now he needed to hire the Lonigans and then take Naoma back with him.

"They'll see you in ten minutes," the barkeep came back and told him.

"Thanks." Obvious the brothers were in the back room and the word "business" had lighted a lamp. In a little while his mission should be completed, then he would convince Naoma to come back to the WTS.

Several men in suits filed out of the back room. They looked like important people and Rafter was taken aback that they would be playing cards in midmorning.

"You can come back now," the bartender said.

Rafter felt their cold, dark eyes on him when he entered the room. A large green felt table centered under a wagon-wheel lamp illuminated the room.

"Mr. Sikes," the thinner-faced brother said as he sat on

the edge of a desk in the corner. "Have a seat. That's my brother, Ike, and I'm Orval."

Rafter eased himself down in the captain's chair at the end of the table.

"What kinda business you got for us?" Ike asked.

"One's a gunfighter showed up down there, the other's a greenhorn college boy. They've took up with the sheep interests."

"You have any names?"

"They aren't hard to pick out at Joseph's Lake. The gunfighter is about six foot, he ain't young, he ain't old. No mustache."

"He got a name?" Ike asked.

"I never heard it said, but he's causing plenty of trouble."

"Like what?"

"Sewed a man's dogs up in sheepskins and sent them home. The man thought they were sheep in his yard and shot them."

Orval turned his face to conceal his amusement. Ike never flinched, he used the side of his index finger to rub under his nose.

"Why can't someone run them down?"

"We're all ranchers."

"So you came up here to get someone to gut-shoot these two clowns?"

Rafter nodded woodenly.

"Cost you five hundred dollars."

"Them dead and gone?"

"We don't get paid for doing stupid things."

"Two fifty now," Rafter said, "and two fifty when they're gone."

"That would work," Ike said, exchanging nods with his brother.

"Fine," Rafter said, relieved the meeting was almost over. He felt like he was in a mortuary planning a funeral. He was in fact doing that for the two troublemakers.

He counted out the money and shoved it across the table. Orval rose, picked it up, and counted it, then nodded at Ike that the money was there.

"When they are dead, we expect prompt payment of the other half," Ike said. His eyes were like deep-burning coals as he waited for the reply.

Rafter agreed and started to rise. He wanted out of this place. It made the skin on his neck crawl to be in the same room with this pair of hardcases.

"A gunfighter and a college man?"

"Yes, sir. I am certain they are the only two like that down there."

"We'll find them. Nice doing business with you, Mr. Sikes."

"Oh, yes," he said, feeling weak-kneed as he stood up and then walked to the door, not certain he would live to get away from them.

In the saloon at last, he savored the smoky air and a wave of relief went through his body. Out of breath, he rested an elbow on the bar and ordered another beer to settle himself. It was over and done. He had just sealed the death warrants on the pair. Easy as that was, if Sam Dugan didn't shut his mouth, he would be next on the Lonigans' hit list. There was no need to take chances. Simply let real killers do it.

"Mister." A big man nudged him and flattened out a wanted poster on the bar.

"You seen this man around here?"

He tried to concentrate on the pen drawing. It could be anyone. He did not recognize it as anyone he had ever seen. Five hundred dollars reward dead or alive. John Slocum, maybe using other aliases. Six foot tall, green eyes, dark hair, works as a dealer sometimes. Consider this man armed and dangerous. Wanted for murder and rape. Contact Sheriff, Fort Scott, Kansas.

"No, can't say that I have." Rafter shook his head. "He suppose to be around here?"

"We tracked him out of Colorado, but we've lost his

trail,'' the big man behind the beard said. His eyes narrowed as he added, ''Me and my brother been after this guy for a long time.''

''Good luck,'' Rafter said, and left the bar, his mind dancing on notions of again fondling the silky-smooth rumps of the two sisters as he climbed the boardwalk. Two of his problems were about to be eliminated. He could afford to spend another day or two in Cedar City before he went back home.

Slocum traded Sam Dugan out of a stout chestnut gelding. He didn't want to ride the Sikeses' horse out of the country without a bill of sale. Besides, he was part of Matty's bill against the Sikeses for shooting the roan he had borrowed from her and she wouldn't let him pay for.

''You're moving on?'' Sam asked with his arms resting on the corral rail.

''Yes, sir,'' Slocum said, busy cinching up his saddle.

''I guess a man who don't let any grass grow under his feet is lucky in a way.''

''How's that?'' Slocum asked.

''You don't ever have to paint no picket fences or get the same dumb cow out of a bog twice.''

''Kinda nice, though, when the north wind blows, to share a bed with an agreeable woman instead of kicking snow off in the morning.''

''Who said a damn thing about having an agreeable woman?'' Then Sam laughed and nodded. ''I know just what you mean. And when you get as old as I am, you'll have to become more serious about finding you that place. I have troubles getting out of bed some mornings, let alone get up off the ground.''

''Takes a big man to ever do what you did up here to make things right with the McArthurs.''

''Takes less to do it right than wrong.'' Sam shook his hand and clapped him on the shoulder. ''You ride careful, Slocum. You did those folks a favor. You're a steady hand even if I was fit to be tied with you over that yearling in the middle of my bed that night.'' Sam shook his head and began to grin. ''Myra's best corset on his head for blinders and him with a case of the loose bowels. You'd of been close, I'd have shot you.''

''I never planned that part.''

''I know. Ride on, amigo,'' Sam said, and waved to him.

He joined Tad and Matty at the store. They had a farm wagon loaded with supplies, a tent for Matty. Tad was driving the team since the rig was too heavy for the two donkeys to pull.

The clear blue sky above, they set out leading two extra saddle horses behind the wagon. Matty on the dun and stirrup to stirrup with Slocum, they headed off the mountain for House Rock Valley.

''You understand that brake?'' Slocum shouted back at Tad.

He nodded. ''I took a course in college on how to do this.'' Then he laughed and dismissed the lie. ''I know she's a steep road going down there.''

Slocum waved that he had heard the man over the clatter of harness, hooves, and the wagon's creak.

''He's offered to go in partners with us in the sheep business,'' she said.

''Well?''

''I think we'll do that,'' she said, looking ahead. ''Unless I can convince someone else—''

''Tad won't make a bad partner.''

Matty acknowledged she had heard him. She never looked his way again. They rode through the pines in silence.

Their descent from the mountain was uneventful save the protesting cry of the brake blocks tight against the iron rims. The locked wheels skidding over rocks and the hard-packed road materials made gritty sounds. Standing up, his foot braced on the dash, Tad sawed the big horses back all the way off the steepest parts. Slocum felt good; the boy would make a hand.

They camped that afternoon near a small spring at the base of the mountain. Another long day lay ahead of them, traveling beside the face of the towering Vermilion Cliffs to the ferry.

A cold wind came up as the long shadow of the plateau spread over the valley floor. Matty's tent set up and the flap from the trailer over the dry sink and cooking things, they gathered under it to eat her beans and dutch-oven biscuits.

"Where will you go next?" Tad asked as they sat on their haunches and ate. Their backs to the wind, they had not spoken much all day.

"I guess like the wild goose, south."

"What's south?"

"Desert mostly, after you get off this high country. Cactus tall as pine trees, everything down there has got thorns on it. You soon buy a pair of thick bullhide chaps to save yourself the spines if you do much riding in it."

"Does it snow?"

"No, but it gets hot enough to cook beans on top of a rock without a fire for half the year."

The shot came from out of nowhere. Tad spun around and grabbed his shoulder. Slocum shoved Matty down as she screamed, "Tad's hit."

Slocum had his Colt in hand as more shots struck the wagon box and others danced in the dirt. He could see the puffs of their rifles on the rise to the south as he reached the Winchester in the wagon.

He sprawled out and began to crease the same rise the gun smoke had appeared on. Two rounds left in the rifle, he paused as Matty joined him.

"How's Tad?" he asked her.

"Just a scratch," Tad shouted. "I'm fine."

"No, he's not," she insisted. "It's a nasty cut across his upper arm."

"Did you get one of them?" Tad asked.

"I doubt it. I can't see anything to shoot at out there."

Above the wind he heard the drum of retreating hooves. They'd run off, the damn cowards

"I think they left," he said, rising, still ready to return any lead at the first sign.

"Lucky shot," Tad said, then he winced as she poured raw whiskey in the cut.

"Can you move your fingers?" Slocum asked. He watched Tad flex a few and nodded in approval. "You'll be all right."

Matty came back with a bandage. "Here, drink some of this." She shoved the bottle at him. "This arm is going to hurt like a sore tooth in a little while."

"Who was that, you reckon, did the shooting?" she asked with a scowl.

"Sikes brothers, I figure. Looked like two riders from the dust I could see."

"Damn, I'm sorry, Tad," she said.

"Hey, I'm grateful they were such damn piss-poor shots."

She and Slocum both chuckled at his words.

"You may make a westerner yet," Slocum said. He rose to his feet and considered chasing the pair, but they were miles away and even on a fresh horse he'd be lost on the vast valley floor with darkness so close at hand. He watched the light fade and wondered if they were alone or the old man had been along. It would be good when the deputy arrived and some sort of justice prevailed. Tad's arm would be sore in the morning, probably should have been sewed shut too. Maybe Emma Lee could do that when they got to the ferry.

He reloaded the Winchester and looked again at the dark hulk of a mountain called Kiabab. If they ever rid the country of Sikes and his boys, it might be one of the best places on earth to ranch.

21

"Paw! Paw, you in there?"

"Who's out there?" Naoma asked as the baby began to cry in the nearby crib. "Someone's pounding on the door like a wild man."

"I know. It's my younger son, Steven," he said, jerking on his pants. What the hell did he want this time of the night? How had he found him anyway?

Naoma had a wrapper around her form and a lamp lighted by the time he had his shirt on. She opened the door as the wide-eyed teen burst in and took a deep gulp at the sight of her.

"I'm looking for—oh, excuse me, ma'am. There you are, Paw. We've got to talk."

"Go out on the porch, I'm coming." He nodded to Naoma that everything would be all right and closed the door behind himself.

"Paw. I'm sorry I come up here at a time like this—"

"Forget that. Whatever is wrong?"

"They've done sent for the law to come from Prescott and arrest all us Sikeses. They're going to pay them

McArthurs back for the lost sheep. And, Paw, Ned and Arland went off to House Rock to kill that gunman, the college man, and her. They sent me up here to find you as fast as I could. I asked and asked all over town trying to find you, and finally some guy said you was up here.''

"You did real good," he said to reassure the boy. He squeezed his mouth in his hand and tried to think out his next move. The Lonigans had his money—two fifty of it. They'd kill the pair of them if his boys hadn't already. But the law coming meant they needed to head west into the back country of the Strip, over around Thunder River. No law with good sense would go in there looking for them.

He'd better hurry while they could still salvage some things to take along with them. Damn, he hated to leave this pair. Daydreaming for a second about their antics with him, he inhaled and shivered, realizing for the first time how cold it was outside, but things were in a serious condition at home. Sam Dugan was a dead man, turning on his own kind like that.

"What we going to do?"

"Get my horse from the stable." He dug some money out of his pocket for the boy to use. "I'll pack my things and be down there in a few minutes."

"Paw."

"Yeah."

"That's her, ain't it?"

"Her?"

"That woman is the one you fell off the bluff for. Going to her place, huh?"

"I guess so, you go ahead."

"Yeah, I won't tell no one."

"Good." He shut his eyes. How much time did he have left? Not much to round up the boys, the horses, things they'd need from the ranch, and to ride.

"Trouble?" she asked when he returned.

"I've got some at home. Damn sheepherders have rooted me out. I may have to start all over again."

"Oh, that's terrible." She shook her head in disappointment. "I was going to ask you for some help too. But I couldn't now, not if you're going to lose your place and all."

"Why, darling, how much did you need?"

She kept her head down and continued to shake it. "I couldn't ask that of you."

"How much?" he insisted.

"Well, I owe over a hundred and I have no money for supplies to take back home with me."

"Two hundred, do you, darling?" He peeled it off his roll and counted it out to her.

"But you said?" She looked at the money in her hands.

"Nothing is too good for you, my darling. Now I'll be coming to see you come springtime. At your little ranch."

"Oh, I'd love for you to come over, Rafter, dear." She jumped up and pulled his head down to kiss him on the mouth.

He finally straightened and slipped on his coat. He saw Rachel, nursing the baby across the room, smile at him.

"And here's twenty to buy that little boy some nice things," he said, and put it on the table.

"Thanks, Rafter," Rachel said.

"In the springtime at my place," Naoma repeated, and hugged his arm going to the door with him. "You be careful. You're too kind, Rafter. Too kind."

"I will be there, and thanks again, girls, for all your hospitality." He drew a deep breath, waved, and then hurried out into the night. Damn, what a mess, the law and all coming down on them. They'd be lucky if some of them didn't do some hard time. But the damn law had to catch them first. Better get their butts out in the back country and quick like though. Things got too hot in the Strip, they could always slip over into Utah. He wasn't doing time ever again in a jail. Two years in Texas behind bars was enough for him—forever.

• • •

Slocum drove the wagon while his sore seatmate Tad tried to act tough. He picked the smoothest stretches of road, but the rocking and the bobbing still jolted the college man's sore arm.

"There's the Colorado." Slocum pointed out the wide red waterway.

"I wasn't impressed when I came across it."

"Too thick to drink, too thin to plow," Slocum said as he used the brake lever on the downhill.

"It is that all right. What's the story on this Lee? He's a polygamist?"

"Six times over, I guess. His first wife is English, nice lady, her name's Emma. Some say John was the leader in the Mountain Meadow Massacre years ago."

"That why he lives way out here and runs a ferry?"

"And to make money off Gentiles."

"What are they?"

"Non-Mormon Christians."

"I have a new name—" He hugged his wounded arm to his side and cringed at the pain.

"Sorry about the hurting."

"I'll be fine. I am not a baby, you know."

"You've done good. I'd ride the river with you."

"That's a strange western terminology. What's it mean?"

"Oh, you can't tell what kind of leather a man's made of until you been on few drives with him or been dragged through some of the things like we've shared.

"I guess cowboys hated those rivers between Texas and Kansas as bad as anything. They lost more hands on those drives to drowning at river crossings and wrecks and the simple fact that they couldn't swim and got separated from their horse. So the toughest job they had was to ride the river, and the best man was one you trusted to try and save your life when the time came."

"I'll ride the river with you anytime, Slocum, anytime."

"I kind of hate to leave you at this point," Slocum said, "but I need to be moving on."

"Oh, I'll be fine in a few days. Besides, I can still use my right arm. And I understand about moving on. Say, I have an uncle in Philadelphia who is one fine lawyer and I'm going to give you his card. You write him sometime and mention me. He is sure knowledgeable about the law and things. Uncle Daniel might just be able to straighten out your past for you."

Slocum accepted the card. Daniel Malone, Attorney at law. He put the card in his vest and thanked him. His gaze was on the turbulent waters of the Colorado at the foot of the hill. Too many trails, too many lies told, he would keep on like that river down there, moving along, though he envied Tad getting to remain with Matty. He wouldn't even mind moving sheep wagons for the rest of his life with her. He knew the two of them would do well together, his business sense and her get-it-done attitude.

Matty came loping back from the outpost store.

"Mrs. Lee wants to look at that wound right away," she said, tightening the chin string from her hat against the sharp wind sweeping down the gorge.

"Get up, ponies," Slocum said, and put them in a trot. "I won't want her to have to wait too long."

At the small store the two women took Tad into the back room. The short English wife of the captain and Matty rushed him along. Seeing he would be of little value, Slocum went outside, took a seat on a log bench out of the wind in the sun, and went to shave on a cedar block with his Barlow jackknife.

The familiar figure of Captain John Lee soon joined him. A short man with a pointed black beard, he wore a starched white shirt and black vest with high top hat. Without a word Lee took a place on the log.

"I thought it was you again. I could almost tell it was you when you drove off the hill." He never looked in Slocum's direction. His hands held the edge of the bench and he squinted as though he were trying to see miles away down the Colorado.

"Been a year or two," Slocum admitted, shaving off another small silver of cedar. "If you can tell me that far away, I guess I'd better change getups."

He shook his head. "Wouldn't be any different. I figure the Lord's going to call us whenever he gets ready."

Slocum nodded he'd heard his words.

"I wasn't here the other day when you came with them about the sheep. The wife recognized you then, so I looked for you to return since you had come from the north this time."

"I guess a lot of men on the move cross here?"

"More than you'd think. I still appreciate you stopping the robbery that day."

Slocum nodded. "I just happened to be handy."

"Those were evil men. If I can ever help you?"

"Thank you, John, I need anything, I'll ask."

"Good." And Lee left.

Slocum crossed his legs and recalled the day that two trail-dusty men dismounted at the store. He had stopped over and was whittling much as he was that day out of sight on the north side because of the summer heat. The two went inside and in a minute held their guns on Lee's wife, Emma, and the children. They began to order them around. They grumbled at her over the small sum of money in the till as they filled pokes with guns, ammunition, and supplies from the stock. They slung them over their shoulders. One of the robbers took a seven-year-old boy as a hostage.

They backed out the door and Slocum stepped in, swept the boy aside, and three guns blazed in close range. The dust settled. One robber was dead, the other died two days later, and all he had were some minor scratches from their bullets striking the adobe and glancing grit off his face.

"Tad's going to be all right if he doesn't get an infection," Matty said, breaking his chain of thought.

"Good."

"Mrs. Lee told us about what a brave thing you did here for her. She wants you to come inside and see her," Matty told Slocum.

"I'll do that," he said, rising to his feet.

He entered the store ahead of Matty, and he saw Emma's short figure as she ran across the floor.

"It's you, me gunnie boy!" Emma hugged him and looked up into his face. "You look well, lad. Still no roots, no good woman. I could find you one, but she'd be a sister in me church, mind you. Aye, she would rub the soreness from your back and bear you lots of children. And, me lad, I can say that no one would tell the authorities that you were there and soon they'd quit looking, right, lad?"

"Emma, I ever want a wife, I'm satisfied you'd find me a good one."

"Oh, I would find you one, lad. A good one too, I might add. And you been helping these two young people, Matty and Tad, they tell me."

"Some. What did you need from me?"

"Well, you know I think that tobacco is the devil's plant?" she whispered.

"Yes, I know that."

"A Gentile came by and was without food for his children and had no money. I would have given him food anyway, but he insisted I take this box." She rose up on her toes and made sure the children weren't privy to her conversation.

"I think you could use it." She handed him the sandalwood box. The sides were so scuffed that the advertising was nearly gone except for the tall Indian who stood on the front, holding a fistful of cigars.

"Good thing you didn't open it," he said, then he hugged her and thanked her. They both laughed until the children frowned at them. He went outside and buried the box in his saddlebag.

"Supper will be ready in a little while," Matty said, intersecting his path.

"Good," he said, and smiled at her. "I'll be right back. A few things I need from the store."

Inside, he bought some beans and crackers to take with him. Emma tried to refuse his money, but he insisted. His supplies tied on his saddle horn, he went to have the last meal with Matty and Tad.

He still had no idea about the direction he should take. The Little Colorado crossing—he could decide later.

22

"Boys, load that stuff faster," Rafter said. He had Arland posted at the main road as a sentry. They were packing and hurrying around in the snow as fast as they could. This trip would be treacherous, but they needed to be gone when the law arrived and there should be no tracks left to follow. It wouldn't be half bad to winter on the Thunder River. Down in the canyon it would be warm and there were some elk to eat as well as mule deer.

Come springtime they could steal enough cattle out of Utah to run in the back country until their brands healed. They might have to move on to Oregon later. No telling, they weren't putting him or his boys in jail, no, sir.

"We've got all we dare take," Ned said.

"I kinda wanted my rocker to go along," he said, looking at the chair he'd brought from Texas.

"What the hell, I'll strap it on," Ned said. He picked it up over his head by the arms and ducked going outside with it.

Rafter could hear the "oh, no" from his youngest, Steven, outside. He looked around. This house didn't have real good memories. About the time they came out to this place was when Barbara quit sleeping in the same bed with him. He never should have brought her from Texas—she was gone anyway, buried outside under the foot or so of snow. He'd never put up with another one like her; it had taken him less than five minutes to smother her to death. He'd listened to her for over twenty years, bitching and telling him this and that.

His bad leg was sore. Riding back from Utah had put a strain on it—the best news he'd heard was they'd hit at least one out of the three in their ambush. Damn shame, they hadn't gotten all three of them.

"We're ready," Ned said, and he followed after him, shutting the door to the house. They might come back sometime, but he doubted it.

He climbed on his bay and never looked back. Ned was already far ahead, taking the lead of the train, and Steven rode midway to line the string out. From the rear he could see his rocker precariously perched on top of a good pack mule.

Slocum crossed the Colorado after supper. Lee's oldest son, Billy, operated the ferry and set him and his horse on the far side. Water lapped against the side of the vessel as he shook the boy's hand, thanked him, and mounted up.

The White Cliffs lined the east side like their counterparts, the Vermilion Cliffs, lined the north side of House Rock. He rode parallel to them on the road the Mormons built and used to migrate down into Arizona. They called it the Honeymoon Trail because so many young couples married and set out on it from Utah for new lands.

After dark he reined the dun off the road and found a place in the junipers and piñons to spread his bedroll beneath the stars. He hobbled the dun and then kicked out the rocks and stubs to make a smooth spot to lay his bedroll on. His boots off, gun belt undone, he still wore his coat, for the night was growing cold. Though there was no snow at this elevation, the wintry chill was unmistakable.

He awoke. Someone was close by. He could hear bells and wondered what was around him. With caution, a hand on his gun butt, he opened one eye. It was daylight and he must have slept hard. A curious brown nanny goat was sniffing him in the face.

He shook his head and drew up on his elbows and discovered all around him were wool goats, some white, some spotted, others brown and a few blacks. They were reared up, browsing on the evergreens and bushes.

" 'Morning, goats," he mumbled, and pulled on his boots from under the cover, where he hoped to keep them warm. He struggled with them in the cold air and finally managed to direct his toe and heel inside the first one, then, while still obsessed with pulling the other one on, he noticed her for the first time. She sat on a rock outcropping not twenty feet away, sipping a cup of coffee.

She wore a colorful woven blanket for a coat, and when she saw he had noticed her, she smiled at him. Her features were very refined and her white teeth were straight.

"Yuta-hey," he said, exhausting his Navaho for hello.

" 'Morning," she said, and blushed, turning her dark eyes away.

"These your goats?"

She nodded.

"Nice goats," he said, and began to roll up his blankets. When he had bound them in a tight roll and tied the strings, he wondered about making himself some coffee.

She had not moved, sitting cross-legged in the sun. Under the traditional blanket she wore a blouse of white muslin and the many-layered skirts of the tribal tradition. With the wrapping over her head and around her, he couldn't tell much about her shape. She was attractive in the face. Well, goat lady, I will return, my bladder is full and I need some sticks to make a fire and—she didn't act like she was going anywhere. Maybe he was on her land. He didn't know.

The goats followed him and bleated a lot. Maybe they

were reporting to her what he was doing. He went back up the hill with several sticks to make a fire. He tossed them down and looked up at her.

"I have coffee, you can drink mine. Come," she said, and rose then, wrapped in the brown and blue blanket.

"Wait," he said, and took up his pad and saddle. He tossed it on the dun, cinched it down, and retied the bedroll on. Finished, he looked at her. He was ready.

With a shrug to adjust her blanket, she started over the hill. First sheep and now goats, with a wary shake of the head he took up the reins and followed her. Slocum, you find more damn things, he berated himself.

She had a canvas tent, two piebald horses staked nearby, and three sleepy-looking burros. Bent over, she held open the flap for him and he ducked to enter. Realizing how nice the small structure was compared to the cold elements outside, he savored the warmth. A small sheet iron stove boasted a kettle and pipe that went through the roof.

She poured him coffee in a cup and indicated he should sit on the rug blanket. Then she placed some fry bread on a wooden plate and served him.

"Thank you. *Gracias*," he added in case she understood Spanish better.

"You are welcome."

"You speak very good English."

She nodded, she understood. Her silver earrings glistened in the light coming through the canvas, and he was shocked by the beauty in her face. Dark as oak, her sculptured facial features made him stare.

"My name is Bet-tay That-way."

He repeated it so he would get it right. "Mine is Slocum."

"Ah, Slo-cum," she said.

"Do you have a husband?"

She shook her head as if to dismiss the notion. Either she was divorced or he was dead. He knew the Navaho and Apache cultures had a hard time speaking of deceased family members. It was bad luck to mention them and they burned or abandoned lodgings that someone had died in.

"I am going to the Little Colorado crossing," he said, eating her fresh fry bread.

She shook her head. "You must go back."

"Why?" He frowned at her over his coffee, still almost too hot to drink.

"The one who is like a teacher will be hurt if you don't go back."

"A teacher?" He looked even harder at her. "You're a medicine woman for your people?"

She nodded.

"And the one you speak of, he is young, tall, and went to college?"

"Yes, young, and tall, and ed-u-cated."

"Who will hurt him if I don't go back?"

"Two men who wear black clothes."

"You saw this?"

"I saw this in my sleep for several nights and knew that you were close by or coming. When I found you I wondered if you would believe me."

He unbuttoned his coat. "I believe you." Witches came in many forms. Bet-tay was one of the powerful ones, but who, coming in black suits, was going to threaten the life of Tad Markum?

"There are others who have your picture on paper."

"Ah, the Abbot brothers." He closed his eyes. They were still behind him after all the tracking and backtracking.

She shook her head; their name meant nothing to her.

"You're telling me I must go back and save this young man and that two bounty hunters are coming after me."

"Yes, I will ride with you."

"What about your goats? And all this?" He frowned at her offer.

"My cousin Bet-tin-ah will come and see after them until I return."

She crossed over and poured him more coffee. "I know many ways to go over there that you don't know. Once my people roamed all this land. Before they let them return from prison, many of the ones who escaped lived across the river during those years."

"Do we have time to stop these men?" he asked.

"Yes, but we must hurry," she said, pulling out her saddle and pads.

He took them from her and went out in the sharp wind. She straightened up outside the tent, pushed the long strands of her free-flowing hair back, and pointed for him to saddle the first horse.

They rode mostly in silence. She wore a bandanna tied tight under her chin against the cold wind and a brown blanket with black lightning designs on it for a coat. All day she acted very intent on reaching the ferry and some destination that she was not sharing with him. He merely rode along, satisfied she knew more about the time frame than he did.

It was at sunset when the ferry came over to get them. Billy acted shocked to see Slocum.

"You're back so soon?" the boy asked

"Yes. Where are Tad and Matty camped?"

"They went out to their sheep camp today."

"Good. There are no strange men at the outpost?"

"No, why?"

"There may be some more men coming." Slocum looked off at the sunset as the water slapped the side of the ferry. "The less they know, the better, about me and those two."

"I'll tell Mother. We won't tell them a thing. You are going to stop and see her?"

"You tell her I will stop next time."

"I will."

The ferry docked, and after he paid the boy, they led their horses up the bank.

"Which way?" he asked her.

"Over the cliffs," she said, pointing in that direction. He shrugged. If there was a way up them from this side, he didn't know it, but a witch should.

She set the black and white horse into a trot up the sandy bank and he waved good-bye to Billy. The light was going fast as he pushed the dun horse after her. Beyond the Lees' peach orchards they rode single file into the shadowy canyon carved into the dark Vermilion Cliffs towering above them. He could see the stars above as he kept the dun close to her horse.

"There is a cabin we can use," she said, twisting in the saddle. "We should be there by midnight."

As his dun hopped up over the ledge of loose rock, he simply hoped that they'd make it there in one piece. Wherever she intended to take them, it looked to him in the dark like a place an eagle might fly to.

23

Rafter looked back, pleased to be on top of the open meadow that stretched for miles. They would need to camp somewhere soon. The trip so far had gone without a hitch. However, they'd never make it to the Thunder River Canyon before dark. He knew the boys didn't want to have to unpack and repack, but they were going to be forced to shut down for the night. If they waited any longer, it would all have to be done in the dark.

He galloped the bay horse through the snow to catch up with Arland.

"Tell Ned that we need to make camp soon."

"Tell him yourself," Arland said. "I consider this a damn foolish move. We could have held off a dozen lawmen at our place."

"What if they brought thirteen?"

"Shit, we'd held them off the same."

"Thunder River, and you won't have to hold off any."

"You always got it all figured, ain't you?" Arland shook his head in disgust.

"Most times, now go tell Ned I said for the two of you to find a camping place."

"This is all horse piss, doing this moving."

"Did you kill that gunman?"

"Hell, I shot to kill him. But it was dark. I hit one of them three good."

"I never heard his name, did you?"

"No, no one ever said it." Arland scratched the side of his head.

"I'd like to know his name. We get set up in the canyon, you and I and Ned need to go shut Sam Dugan's mouth permanent like."

"Do it now!"

"Tell Ned—"

"I know, we need to camp somewhere in this ice field."

"Yes." He reined his horse aside to get back to the rear and drive the few stragglers along. He'd stand a better chance catching Sam in a crossfire with those two. They wanted killings, he'd take them along on several before this winter was over. There would be blood on the snow, and lots of it.

Ned, he could see, had ridden ahead to scout for a place for them to camp. Good, he could stand to get off this horse, his leg had been throbbing all afternoon. He hadn't said a word, but he was ready to turn in.

Slocum dropped heavily from the saddle, past midnight by his count. He undid the girth, lifted rig and pad and all, then he released the dun, knowing that he would be close in the morning.

"I'll do that," he said to Bet-tay as she loosened her rig. She dismissed him. They pushed inside the shack out of the night wind and dropped their gear on the floor. He struck a match and held it high, casting long shadows of a table and crude chairs. The next lucifer he struck he applied to the small candle in a jar on the table. Grateful, the last user had stored the stub, or else a pack rat would have eaten it by then, he felt certain. The wavering lamp showed the logs had been chinked, and it held two cots and a small wood heater and a few chunks of juniper to burn.

"Whose place is this?" he asked, his breath rolling out in steamy vapors.

"A miner's," she said, and spread her bedding on the near cot.

"Did he find anything?"

"No," she said, and straightened. "We have only a few hours to sleep."

"Yes, ma'am," he said, and went to make his place. She was a taskmaster all right. There were lots of questions about this mystery woman he would like to ask. But for the time being he would trust her knowledge about the unfolding events.

He had barely shut his eyes when he heard her chucking wood in the stove. Short night on top of the cliffs. He rose and pulled on his boots, grateful for the cot despite the fact he still felt as sleepy as he had before he slept.

"Saddle the horses, we'll take time for coffee," she said, as she knelt down to blow the fire alive in the stove.

"Yes, ma'am," he said, and slipped on his hat. He caught the horses, thinking that they'd now be able to head off the killers. The wind had grown sharper overnight, it seemed as he led them back. It would be a cold day to ride, he mused, as he studied the faint pink horizon still untouched by the sun.

"Will we get there in time?" he asked, coming inside.

"I think so," she said, looking up at him as she sat at the table wrapped in her blanket.

"Two men in suits?" he asked. "Two men with beards? Together?"

"No, the men in suits want you and the ed-ucated man and the white woman. The bearded ones want you."

He held his hands to the stove, feeling the first heat as the juniper wood began to crackle inside. "The bearded men are from Fort Scott, Kansas, they are the Abbot brothers. They have a picture?"

She nodded.

"I wish I knew the killers in the suit, unless Sikes hired them?" He spoke his thoughts out loud.

She turned her palms up. He drew up a chair and faced her across the table.

"You know these men's faces?"

"Oh, yes."

"Good. We can be at Joseph's Lake by dark if we ride. Barney McKey will tell us if they've been through there or not."

"I think we should wait at the Seven Springs," she said.

"At the base of the mountain?"

"Fine, we'll wait there." He, at least, knew her destination. They could ride there, he felt certain, in a half day. Good, something was settled.

The coffee tasted luxurious. They finished the last of it, mounted up, and headed west through the juniper and piñons. He turned in the saddle and noticed how the log cabin had blended out of sight. Either he was on the path of the ghost Navahos who had evaded Kit Carson's roundup, or this was the much-talked-about outlaw trail that led to Mexico. Perhaps both paralleled this way. A much less obvious route than the Mormon road across House Rock Valley.

They arrived at the springs and no one was there. She looked around for any sign in the grounds, holding the horse rein, and shook her head. Several pockets of water in the mud were frozen over.

"No one has been here," she said, and swung up on her horse in a lithe swing.

"We go camp up in the trees?" he asked with a toss of his head.

"Good," she agreed.

He wondered if they dared light a fire. They might freeze their butts off waiting for the two killers, but whatever she could stand, he could too.

She soon had a fire made to satisfy him, though they kept their horses saddled and hobbled so they would be close. Under a blanket he sat cross-legged and absorbed the warmth while he wished the distant sun had more power.

"When did you learn you were a witch?" he asked.

"I dreamed one night the soldiers were coming to Canyon De Shay. I told my mother and my father. They went and saddled our horses and took our goats, and we left. Others, they laughed and said we were only afraid. The soldiers would never find that place. Two days, Colonel Carson came and took them all away."

"Did you begin to understand your powers then?"

"No, not until a man came to see me. He was an Apache medicine man. He had heard of my dreams, I was perhaps eighteen and he said he wanted to marry me. I would not marry an Apache, even a powerful medicine man. They are not easy people, the way they live on the move all the time. But he stayed for many days and asked me many questions about my dreams."

"Did you see him in your dreams?"

"Oh, yes, I told him a bullet would never take his life. I saw him as an old man who had many young wives and he would be growing pumpkins and melons. He asked me about the last part over and over—growing pumpkins, not being at war, worried him."

"What was his name?" he asked.

"Gotholay—white men call him Geronimo."

Slocum figured that the two killers would arrive about noontime. He assumed that if they stayed overnight at Joseph's Lake, it would be midday or later before they reached the springs. While the natural spring tanks were off the road, they were a favorite stopover point. Most everyone came by them and watered their horses. The next watering hole was a good five hours' ride east.

Nevertheless, the two of them waited in the deep cold, replenishing their fire and listening. Maybe the deep freeze had forced the pair to change their plans, he couldn't help but think. A couple of hours snaking in some firewood, it could be toasty inside. He gave a shiver and hauled the blanket up over his shoulder.

Late in the evening he quit splitting up dry wood when he heard riders approaching. Bet-tay had been busy with something all afternoon. He simply figured it was witch business, and so he kept warm chopping wood.

"Stay here," she said to him. "I have a plan. Do not let them see you." He couldn't see much, but he could make out two men leading a packhorse coming from the road. He wondered for a long while if they were the Abbot brothers or the men in suits that she spoke of.

"Howdy there, squaw," one of the men said.

She did not answer, just sat there on the ground, wrapped in her blanket. Slocum remained out of sight, but drew his pistol, in case they tried to hurt her in any way.

"Tell me something, injun. We're looking for three folks. An eastern dude called Tad, a gal who owns sheep, and a gunman whose name is Slocum, they said back at the store."

"Maybe they sick," she said, her head still down. "White people and injuns all sick down here."

Orval reached over and whipped back the blanket from her face. "What the hell's the matter with—" He staggered back at the sight of her. Slocum tightened his grip on the pistol, unable to see what was wrong.

"Sweet Jesus, man, she's got the damn smallpox!" Ike shouted, and they both panicked for their horses. "We've got to get the hell out of here! She said that everyone down here had it!"

"Hell, for what little he paid us, it ain't worth dying over."

Slocum watched them beat their horses and clamber up the mountain for Joseph's Lake. They wouldn't stop until they got to Utah, maybe even Salt Lake City.

He holstered the pistol and came over to her. She was laughing as she knelt at the spring and washed the telltale makeup from her face. He hugged her shoulder, pleased with the outcome. She rose and took his face in her hands and kissed him hard on the mouth. He winked at her, pleased with her well-laid plans.

When they stood apart, he checked and listened for the sounds in the twilight—he could still hear them far away, shouting and whipping their horses to escape the smallpox epidemic.

"I have a few more to round up," he said decisively. "Only one person hired those two, Rafter Sikes, and I think he killed his wife. I'm not sure how he did it, but I think he killed her. If I could prove it, it would sure make me happy."

"Who is this man?" she asked.

"A madman. I never could figure why he didn't bury that woman and left her for us to do it. Maybe his leg was hurt too badly. I still wonder."

"What will we do?"

"I'm not sure, it will be dangerous and I don't want you hurt. We need to bring them in for the law," Slocum said, unsure how they would ever manage.

"Where is he?"

"Maybe at his ranch far to the south." He paced back and forth. Matty, Tad, and he had convinced the cattle people to quit. Could the two of them convince the Sikeses to surrender?

"Let's bring them in," she said.

"Yes," he said, and hugged her. "We are going to gather them up."

They reached the deserted ranch house the next afternoon. The tracks told him everything. They found some foodstuff left, and firewood, and soon had the living room warmed. He hauled water inside for a bath and to shave. He dragged out the tub and set it close by the fireplace.

Bet-tay made fry bread from the flour that the Sikeses had overlooked in their haste. They sat together on the floor before the warm fire and sipped coffee, enjoying being truly warm for the first time in days.

"Damn nice of old Sikes to leave us this place," he said, and then he kissed her.

She moved her mouth away and looked at the fire. "He is maybe a day's ride from here in a canyon."

"You have seen him?"

She nodded thoughtfully. "Four of them." Then they kissed hard and she sprawled under him with a smile. "You are much fun to ride with, Slocum."

24

"Paw, come quick!" Steve shouted from the door. The boy's face was as white as a sheet. He held the door wide open and trembled where he stood frozen in place.

"What the hell is wrong?"

"Maw's out there!" He pointed, and Rafter blinked at the figure beside the pine tree across the stream.

Rafter swallowed hard. How could it be her? He'd smothered her damn bitching mouth with a pillow until she was dead.

"Hey!" he shouted, and the figure did not move.

"It's a trick, son," he said, having a hard time keeping from shaking. That would be a dead giveaway, him trembling 'cause he saw his murdered wife. His boys never found her to bury her. It hurt when he swallowed again and began to advance across the yard. That thing wasn't real. The dress and the coat and the scarf, they were hers, but how the hell did they get there?

He sloshed through the water with Steven beside him, his heart racing a thousand beats a minute. He reached for the figure and jumped back screaming with all his might when her head rolled off.

"Paw! Paw!" Steven was beating him on the shoulder and jerking his arm. "Quit screaming! It ain't real. It's a damn dummy."

"Yeah, yeah," he said, sweeping his hair back and gasping for air. His knees were shaking so badly, they would hardly hold him. He saw the face painted on the material, the eyes were open, and the mouth was a straight line. Whoever had made it had seen her in death.

"Paw, come look."

"What did you find?"

"Don't them prints look like Maw's?"

He looked in the untramped snow at the prints leading toward the barn. They were a woman's boot tracks. None of the boys had had feet that small for years. Had she come back to haunt him? He'd kill her again if he had to. But how could she be back? She couldn't! It was Matty who had done this.

"You sum bitches, I'll get all of you!" he screamed. "All of you!"

"Paw, who do you figure is behind this?"

"That damn gunman and the girl. Like the sheep tricks."

"Oh, we'll get them," Steven said. "We'll set some traps."

Take more than traps. They were smart, they'd tricked some smart ranchers. He had to stop shaking first. What did they know about Barbara's death? Had he said anything around Steve to draw suspicion?

"Paw, come inside, the boys will be back from hunting in a day. You're shivering bad, you better get inside or you'll have pneumonia."

"Who's out there?" Arland asked, trying to see beyond their campfire.

"I am cold," she said.

"Who in the hell are you?" He squinted to see the willowy figure. He rose up on his knees with the Winchester in his right hand. "Damn, who are you?"

She moved in closer and raised her skirt higher for him to gaze at her shapely legs.

"You damn sure ain't Matty. Come in here." He stood up and started around the fire to see more of her. When he was close enough, she jammed the derringer in his ribs and then, wordless, led him away from the fire.

"Nice to see you," Slocum said, holding his hands behind his back.

"You won't get away with this."

"Lower your voice," Slocum said, pushing him down on the snow to sit. "You make one sound, you'll be gagged."

"The other one is asleep," she said, squatting beside him as he bound Arland's feet.

"He's next."

"I'll freeze out here like this," Arland said.

"Should have worried about that a long time ago. Like before you two raped that girl," Slocum said as Arland batted his eyes in disbelief.

With a toss of his head they crossed the snow. With no effort they awoke Ned with a pistol pressed to his ear and captured the other hunter.

"What do you have in mind for us?" Ned asked as Slocum tied him up.

"The judge can decide when he comes to Joseph's Lake. The charges are rape, attempted murder, threatening and killing sheep."

"You ain't the law."

"We are making citizen's arrests."

"This is bullshit. I thought the old man hired them Lonigans to blow his ass to kingdom come?" Ned asked his tied-up brother.

"Shut up, Ned," Arland said with a defeated look.

"Don't count on them, boys. We've already set a roman candle to their butts and they're in Utah or farther away." Slocum and Bet-tay laughed.

"Who in the hell is she?"

"Bet-tay, she's a medicine woman."

"A what?"

"A witch."

"Hell, there aren't any witches, are there, Arland?"

"Shut up, Ned, this whole damn thing ain't getting any better. You spilling your guts."

They arrived at the Joseph's Lake store. Slocum stayed up in the timber with his prisoners. Bet-tay went ahead to speak to Barney McKey and be certain that the Abbot brothers weren't in there. In a few minutes Barney came on the run, putting on his coat and wool cap.

"You got two of them, huh?" He shook his head in amazement.

"You've got to hold them until the law comes or send them to Prescott."

"We can do that. When you bringing in the old man?"

"When I can prove he murdered his wife."

"Paw never done nothing like that—" Arland blurted out.

"What makes you so damn sure?" Slocum asked.

"I know him," Arland said, straining at the tight bindings Slocum had knotted onto the saddle horn.

"Something damn suspicious about how she died," Slocum said.

"If he killed her, why I'd kill him with my bare hands," Arland said.

"I'd help him," Ned added.

Slocum looked at the two and then wondered—had the man murdered his wife? Why did he feel so strong about the matter?

"They're your prisoners, Barney."

"May I have a word with you?"

"Certainly," Slocum said, and stepped down. They walked a few yards, to where they could speak and the Sikeses could not overhear them.

"Them Lonigans was here about five days ago. They

said some injun woman in House Rock had smallpox and said everyone else down there had it too.''

"Did they go home?"

"Oh, hell yes, that day. You do know them guys are real killers.''

"Yes, I know. Bet-tay tricked them into believing she had smallpox. Sikes had hired them to kill Tad and me.''

"What else? Good to know there ain't no smallpox down there. We didn't need smallpox up here or down there. We'll watch these jaspers real close.''

They headed back. Even though it was out of the way, Slocum planned to use the Sikeses' ranch house so they would have one night out of sleeping in the snow and ice.

Long past dark they put their horses in the pens, fed them grain from the bins, and hurried though the cold night to the dark house. Inside he set his bedroll aside and lit a candle. Bet-tay stayed close by him as he built the fire in the hearth. He rather enjoyed her closeness, but was unclear why. Nothing in the old house did he consider as a threat— maybe a pack rat, but they were man-friendly.

The fire began to blaze, and he turned and kissed her. The warmth swept out of the fireplace as they knelt before it together. He untied her head scarf when he noticed the tear leaking from her eye.

"What makes you sad?" He thought she would enjoy a night of their making love as well as sleeping before the roaring fire.

"I know now how he killed her." Her upper arms trembled as he held them.

"When did you know about it?"

"When we came inside the house tonight. She told me.''

"How did he do it?" he asked, looking into the deep pools of brown.

"With a pillow over her face.'' She hugged him tightly and buried her face in his neck.

25

Rafter stood up straight and blinked into the early morning light. Dangling in the open doorway on a string hung a pillow. He frowned and searched around, eager to get outside and relieve himself. He couldn't imagine who had strung a damn pillow right in his way. He pushed past it and went ten steps before he undid his pants. What the hell kind of a joke was this? He glanced around with a frown. A prank?

That damn gunfighter and that McArthur bitch were back at their tricks. But how did they know about the pillow? They couldn't know a damn thing. Why would they hang the damn thing in the doorway? Some kind of a trick, he was sure, he slipped back into the house and closed the door carefully so as not to disturb the thing as the wind swept it back and forth like a pendulum. Sum bitches, he'd show them some damn buckshot when they came back.

Arland and Ned were still out hunting. Hell, the weather hadn't been all that bad. Them oldest boys—something had happened to them. They should have been back days ago. He and the boy better go looking for them.

"Steven, Steven." He looked across the room and saw the boy's bedcovers had been turned back, but it was empty. How had they gotten him? Was he outside somewhere? When Steven went out, they must have grabbed him. He jerked up the shotgun, threw open the door, and blasted the pillow with both barrels in a fury.

"I'll get you three!" He kicked the door shut. Damn them, they all needed killing. That gunman, whatever his unholy name was. Funny, he'd never heard. Those Lonigans wasn't as tough as they were made out to be, or he wouldn't be in all this damn trouble at this very minute. No, sir, he might just go back up there and demand his money back. They were simply a pair of crooks taking his last dollars and then not lifting a finger to get rid of that gunfighter and the dude.

Come night, he'd slip away from this cabin and they would never find him. No one knew this Colorado gorge like he did. What had they done with his boys? They'd do some hard time if that girl spoke up about them raping her. He wasn't doing any jail time, no, sir. After dark he was getting the hell out. It was every man for himself from here on.

"Rafter? We know you killed your wife with a pillow. Better confess!"

"Confess, hell!" he shouted. "She died of a heart attack."

"We know better."

"You can't prove a damn thing!" he yelled back.

"She told us you did it."

"When you got there, she was deader than a doornail!" he said, trying to figure where they were located at outside. Moving, they were all over out there.

"You smothered her under that pillow."

"She never told you that!"

"You know you did it!"

He searched around. They were outside somewhere, and with only one small window in the front of the cabin he couldn't tell exactly where they were. If he could get them in his sights, he'd shoot hell out of them. No way that they were trapping him into admitting he'd killed her. Beside the door he spotted the bar and quickly crossed the room and put it in place. At least they couldn't bust in on him now.

"You killed her. Just admit it. We know."

He was silent.

"You wanted the money she had hidden. She wouldn't give it to you, so you killed her."

"Lies! Damn lies! She never had no money."

"You killed her, didn't you?"

He didn't bother to answer. He needed to get away after dark. He wished he could smother that accuser to death. Must be the gunman, the talker didn't have an eastern accent. Back and forth he paced the floor like a trapped grizzly.

Noontime, it had begun to snow. Slocum shook his head as he stood under the shed roof and watched the flakes fall. Bet-tay stood close by. If they tried to rush the cabin, someone would die. Sooner or later Sikes would have to come out. However, the storm pushing in might trap them in the canyon for weeks and their supplies weren't sufficient for a long siege. His plan to get the man to confess within hearing of his own son had not panned out. He hated that the most. The bound youth never looked at either of them.

"Let's saddle up and take the boy to Joseph's Lake. Then we won't be trapped here if the weather gets worse. Rafter Sikes isn't going far. A posse can come up here and get him anytime before spring."

"We'll take all the horse stock?" she asked.

"Good idea. Leaving him here afoot isn't a bad idea. His bad leg isn't going to carry him far."

Long past dark that evening Slocum, along with Bet-tay, spoke on the back porch of the store with Barney McKey. Their prisoner was lodged in the new log jail with his kinfolk. The white flakes fell at a leisurely rate as the three of them huddled in the dark shadows behind the store to visit.

"When the law comes, we'll go up and round up Rafter," Barney promised. "Save us feeding him until the trial."

"The law ain't come yet?" Slocum asked.

"I've got a letter, They're coming next week on a circuit through here and said for me to hold all prisoners. The county is paying twenty-five cents a day keep on them."

"Good. We need some things. Two pounds of coffee, five pounds of beans, that much rice, some raisins, ten pounds of flour, baking soda, lard," Slocum listed.

"Come in and pick it out. Ain't no one in the store, folks kinda drifted home early when the snow began." Barney pushed open the back door.

"Guess we'll claim one of those pack mules of Sikes'," Slocum said.

"Be small enough reward for all the work you've done for folks up here," Barney agreed. "Guess you hadn't heard, but Matty and that dude Tad are going to get hitched when the judge gets here."

"Good," Slocum said as he piled the extra things on the counter. He considered saying more, but decided to let the matter ride. They had each other. Then he recalled reining his horse back in the trees as the blond-haired Butler woman drove by. Matty wasn't his anymore either.

"I meant to tell you. You know them two Abbot brothers was through here asking about a man called Slocum?" Barney said. "Don't know why I forgot to tell you. Anyway, no one up here had ever heard of him. They went on east to the ferry about three days ago."

"Thanks," Slocum said.

"Aren't you two going to spend the night?"

"No, we better get on off the mountain," Slocum said, looking at Bet-tay for the answer.

She gave a sharp nod.

"Folks up here won't ever forget you and all you did for us."

"Good. Now figure up the bill."

"Nope, I'm charging the county enough for those prisoners. You take it."

"Barney, I have close to ten dollars worth of food here." He looked the man in the eye. There was way too much for him to accept the supplies as a gift.

"And two good bottles of whiskey," Barney added as he showed off his addition. "It's yours from everyone on the mountain. I'll help you saddle that mule with a pack saddle if you'd like, and then we'll load this up."

"Stay here, where it's warm, for a while," Slocum said to her.

She smiled and agreed.

When daylight came the snow was down to a powdery fall. After riding all night, they finally reached the cabin on the Vermilions. He kicked loose some firewood piled outside. His arms full of fuel, he followed her inside.

"Those bounty men won't ever find us here," she said.

Good, he had a witch's promise. He leaned over and kissed her cold lips.

"I don't figure anyone will find us up here for the next couple months."

"Months?" she asked, closing her right eye as if to gauge his time frame.

"Months," he repeated, down on his knees, shedding his gloves to start a fire, a roaring blaze, one hotter than the summer sun. He watched her knee-high boots cross the room—months might not be long enough. Who knew?

Epilogue

Slocum's friend, John Doyle Lee, was arrested in November 1874 and tried the following April for his role as a leader in the Mountain Meadow Massacre. The jury was hung, so he was held over for another trial. Released on bond in spring 1876, he came back, was tried again, and found guilty of all the murders and atrocities of the Mountain Meadow Massacre. He was denied by his own church, excommunicated, and given six months to confess to the court. He wrote a bitter diary about his betrayal by cowards, including Mormon church elder Brigham Young, and on March 23, 1877, he was executed by a firing squad at the site of the crime.

Emma Lee and her children continued to operate the ferry for a number of years after Lee's death. Billy Lee, the eldest, worked as hard as a man despite his young age to provide this very necessary service for travelers.

Rafter Sikes escaped the posse, and the following year, at Silver City, New Mexico, he was hung for horse thieving. Ned and Arland each served one year in Yuma Territorial Prison for their parts in the range war. However,

Coconino County court records never showed that the charge of rape was ever drawn up against the pair.

In 1884, Ned Sikes was shot to death by a bartender during an altercation in the Hell Hole Saloon in Phoenix. Arland Sikes died of old age and infirmities in the Pioneer Home in Prescott, Arizona, in 1922. The charges against Steven, due to his young age at the time of their trial, were dismissed, and he was last known farming in Oregon with a wife and four children.

Matty and Tad Markum became prominent ranchers and later were active in the retail business when they moved their headquarters to Flagstaff, Arizona. A thirty-two-degree Mason, Tad died in 1910 from injuries received in a runaway buggy accident. Matty expired in her sleep in 1932. The three Markum children were active in state politics.

If you enjoyed this book, subscribe now and get...

TWO FREE

A $7.00 VALUE—

If you would like to read more of the very best, most exciting, adventurous, action-packed Westerns being published today, you'll want to subscribe to True Value's Western Home Subscription Service.

Each month the editors of True Value will select the 6 very best Westerns from America's leading publishers for special readers like you. You'll be able to preview these new titles as soon as they are published, *FREE* for ten days with no obligation!

TWO FREE BOOKS

When you subscribe, we'll send you your first month's shipment of the newest and best 6 Westerns for you to preview. With your first shipment, two of these books will be yours as our introductory gift to you absolutely *FREE* (a $7.00 value), regardless of what you decide to do. If

you like them, as much as we think you will, keep all six books but pay for just 4 at the low subscriber rate of just $2.75 each. If you decide to return them, keep 2 of the titles as our gift. No obligation.

Special Subscriber Savings

When you become a True Value subscriber you'll save money several ways. First, all regular monthly selections will be billed at the low subscriber price of just $2.75 each. That's at least a savings of $4.50 each month below the publishers price. Second, there is never any shipping, handling or other hidden charges—*Free home delivery*. What's more there is no minimum number of books you must buy, you may return any selection for full credit and you can cancel your subscription at any time. A TRUE VALUE!